1 The Big Day

I held up the diamond ring in front of her face, letting the gem's crystal facets scatter light in every direction. My heart beat rapidly and a tight knot formed in my throat.

The bland holiday muzak playing on the speakers over our heads did nothing to calm my nerves. The big moment, the one I dreamt of and sweat about for weeks, had finally arrived. I had made up my mind. I would go through with it. I would take the chance. I had looked and looked and looked, and now I would leap.

I finally looked away from the ring and into her bright, questioning blue eyes. She cocked her head to one side and gazed back steadily at me. A smile curved the corner of her lip and she raised an eyebrow, waiting to hear what I would say next.

"Can I ask you a favor?" I asked.

"Of course," she replied, tilting her head the other way and raising both eyebrows curiously, still smiling with an expression of mixed curiosity and amusement.

"Would you put this on?" I asked.

She lifted her slender hand toward me and I slid the ring onto her finger. It fit perfectly. It looked stunning. She tilted her hand back and forth slowly, letting each of the diamond's facets shatter the light, sparkling like the afternoon sun painting ocean ripples with a trillion undulating stars.

"Is today the day, then?" she asked, smiling sweetly again.

I began to raise my head to nod yes, when something tightened again around my heart. The same familiar…something. Was I just nervous? I never expected to get cold feet over buying a ring and asking Julie to marry me. I always thought it would be the most natural thing in the world, a perfectly happy moment.

But every time I came so close to deciding, something would knot up inside and stop me. I wanted to ignore it. I wanted to just push through my irrational, senseless fear. I could never ask for a more perfect girl. I'd be a fool to pass up this chance.

"Hello, Spencer," the store manager said, walking past me. "Admiring the ring again, I see. Are you taking it home today?"

"I've never seen him so close, Ron," Holly answered. She lowered her hand to the glass showcase, then slipped the ring from her finger and replaced it in its velvet-covered box.

"I know you can afford it, Spencer," Ron said, stepping behind the counter and next to the salesperson. "And you obviously love the girl. So what's stopping you?"

I opened my mouth to answer, but nothing came out and I merely shrugged.

"Tell you what I'm going to do for you," Ron said, leaning on the glass and giving me a direct stare. "You put a deposit down on the ring. Make your first payment today and sign an agreement. If she says no, you bring it right back in and I'll give you a full refund. No questions asked."

"That's very generous of you, Ron," I said. After all the time I had spent in the store, we were all on a first-name basis. "I appreciate it, but I was planning to ask her over Christmas break, and we'll be out of town for a couple weeks."

"No problem," he answered, waving off my objection. "I trust you."

I looked down at the ring once more. It was perfect. For the perfect girl. And now there was no financial risk in taking the ring. I had no more objections, and I was running out of time. Finals would end tomorrow and then I'd leave town for Christmas vacation.

I reached into my back pocket and pulled out my wallet, then handed a credit card to Holly. "Ring it up," I told her.

"That's what they all say," Holly responded with a wry smile.

With the decision made, the knot around my heart loosened. I suddenly couldn't wait to put my new plan into action. Once Julie and I got together for Christmas, everything would work out perfectly.

Holly walked over with some paperwork. "Two signatures, Spencer, and you'll be on your way."

I signed the papers, thanked Holly and Ron, and stepped out into the mall concourse. Holiday music piped over the speakers. I wanted to run, not walk, out to my car to drive home. I slipped the small box into my pocket and nearly skipped along.

The hard part had passed. I had taken the one difficult step into commitment and everything would be downhill from this point forward.

In a way that I'd never have guessed in a million years, I was exactly right.

The Perfect Gift

by Shaun Roundy

OVERVIEW

The sequel to the popular and insightful novel *Courage, Love and the Meaning of Christmas*, *The Perfect Gift* picks up with our main characters Spencer, Ski and many others one year later.

In *Courage, Love and the Meaning of Life*, Spencer discovered the Meaning of Life and fell in love with the girl of his dreams.

Knowing the Meaning of Life doesn't help much, however, if you're unable to apply it.

This year it's Ski's turn for a miracle. This year, it's Ski's turn to experience an amazing personal transformation. This year, you will learn how to overcome your own private challenges on the deepest level possible...with a little help from Upstairs, naturally.

Can people ever really change? You'd better hope so.

The Perfect Gift doesn't begin as you may have expected. Much has changed in the past year, but not nearly as much as is about to. What doesn't change is the engaging, thrilling, funny, profound, touching, inspiring, plot-twisting, enjoyable holiday reading.

Dedicated to
Everyone
who suffers
invisible wounds.

A CHRISTMAS
ADVENTURE-ROMANCE
NOVEL

BOOK ONE: COURAGE, LOVE &
THE MEANING OF CHRISTMAS
BOOK TWO: THE PERFECT GIFT
BOOK THREE: THE ART OF HEART

2nd Edition
© 2023 The University of Life Press
ISBN 978-1-893594-18-0

2 Happiness

On the drive home I reviewed my plans. Just yesterday Julie had agreed to spend Christmas break with me in Wyoming. Now the details would fall into place automatically.

First we'd ride snowmobiles or cross-country ski until we were completely alone, miles and miles from anyone and anywhere. I'd turn to her and put one arm around her waist. She would wrap her arms around my neck and draw close until our faces nearly touched. Then I would kiss her, and as she closed her eyes, I would reach into my coat pocket and take out the ring. When she opened her eyes, the ring would be right there waiting and then our new life together would begin.

Or perhaps we would wait until everyone at Grandma's had gone to sleep. We would sit up together on the couch in front of a gently flickering fire. We would talk about anything and then fall into a peaceful silence, holding each other close. "I have a question for you," I'd announce. She would look up at me and I would pull out the ring. After a proper proposal, she would be mine, I would be hers, and together we would live happily ever after.

It didn't really matter how it happened. That moment would be only the beginning.

Such daydreams continued to fill my mind until three hours later while trying to study in the Student Center. The couch where I sat felt comfortable, but I shifted restlessly and couldn't focus on my textbook. After reading the same paragraph at least a dozen times with no comprehension, I slammed it shut and stood up. I needed a break. I walked downstairs to the food court and bought a cup of hot chocolate, then headed outside to sit in the cold air and sunshine.

I had been sitting with my eyes closed for less than two minutes when a snowball hit my shoulder and almost made me spill the steaming cup in my hand. A bit of the snow bounced into my coat collar and began to melt against my neck, but I didn't move to brush it out. I knew who had thrown the snowball and my part of this game was to pretend I didn't notice and give him the least possible satisfaction.

Footsteps drew near the table. "Hey, Ski," I said coolly with my eyes still closed. I only opened them when it occurred to me how easily he could shove a handful of snow down my coat, and then pretending to ignore the cold would be pointless. Everything was a game with Ski.

"What's up?" he asked, taking a seat at the table. He wore a black ski jacket and a fleece hat that attached with velcro below his chin.

I sipped my hot chocolate after dropping in a small chunk of snow from my shoulder into the steaming cup to cool it down. Ski smiled just a bit, admiring the casual way I had turned his attack to my advantage. Chalk up one point for me.

We sat in silence for a minute longer and he asked again. "What's up?" I looked back at him without answering, a slight smile on my lips. He leaned back in his chair, watching me casually.

Behind his calm exterior, I knew his mind was racing, spinning, searching for whatever meaning my silence communicated. He sometimes reminded me of Sherlock Holmes, and I often felt like Dr. Watson. After watching me for a moment longer, he turned and looked casually around the patio as if he had lost interest.

"Well, it's about time," he said in his most blasé tone of voice.

"How'd you know?" I asked

"It's obvious," he answered, looking back at me. "Your stupid, happy grin gives you away."

My stupid, happy grin grew even wider. Ski knew me better than anyone. We hadn't seen a lot of each other lately despite being roommates this year, but he knew about the decision I had been trying to make over the past several weeks.

He didn't look as happy for me as I expected. He usually told me that I should just buy the ring and get on with proposing, that Julie was perfect and she loved me and I was a fool for hesitating.

Ski had been instrumental in getting us together in the first place, nearly a year ago. Even though I had a serious crush on her for an entire semester, Julie had, At first,, only been interested in Ski. He claimed that she wasn't his type, though, and he talked me up so much that she finally turned her attention in my direction. From there, everything fell into place naturally.

I leaned back in the cold metal chair and took a deep breath, feeling very optimistic about the future. "Well," I said, "one more day, then one more semester, then graduation and we're done with all this." I raised my styrofoam cup in a toast to the university and let the steam rise into the cold, dry December air. "And then we head out into the real world."

"Yeah, *then* we'll be happy," Ski replied.

He usually said this to provoke well-meaning people into

serious little lectures about how you have to choose to be happy *now*, at *this* moment, and not wait for some magical future event to create your happiness. He would listen with wide eyes and mock interest, encouraging them, nodding his head and saying "Hmm" and "Uh huh" and "I never thought of it that way" from time to time. The bright ones would catch on to his sarcasm and mumble a quick finish, sometimes even stopping mid-sentence and showing their disdain for his rudeness with a disgusted sneer.

This was the kind of game Ski played whenever he got the chance. A kind of battle of wits that made everyone else look like an idiot. I had learned to play along and enjoy the games, though I often told him, sincerely, what a jerk he was.

As for happiness, Ski had his own opinions. He had opinions about everything. "There's no such thing," he sometimes said. What I always thought he meant was that there's no such thing as the magical, easy, blissful Cinderella kind of dream-life that most people wish for. "Lower your expectations and you'll rarely be disappointed," he counseled.

I usually disagreed with him, of course, but never minded listening to his cynical commentaries on life. Sometimes I'd argue, and by the time the ensuing discussion slowed down, neither of us would have changed our positions, but my opinions would have become more clearly defined. Talking with Ski was like hammering a chisel against a giant granite block. Chip by chip, I found my perceptions about the world emerging from the once-shapeless mass.

And I enjoyed the games. They were fun. Fun to get my brain moving at that speed, fun to think thoughts that had never before entered my mind, fun to laugh at the world's idiosyncrasies that Ski had such a knack for noticing and pointing out.

"So when *will* you be happy?" I asked. Fall Semester was almost over, we had known each other for over a year now, and while he laughed often enough and never lacked for energy and enthusiasm to fuel his cynical humor, I realized that he never did seem truly happy. His laughter was never the kind that penetrated all the way down inside, as if all his laughter came from his throat and not his stomach.

I expected my question to be a thought-provoking one and was surprised by how quickly he answered.

"Oh, I won't," he said quickly. "I'll never be happy."

My brain spun into high gear as I tried to decipher his meaning. Did he mean he never expected to find a fairy-tale life?

Did he mean that he recognized the need for continual effort and struggle in order to continue growing? "What about the easy way?" I asked.

'The easy way' was what Ski called learning and awareness. He said that nothing has to be hard if you're willing to *learn*. He said that if you *watch* and ponder, you'll learn all you need to know. And if you learn something, if you come to truly, deeply understand it, then nothing will seem hard to do or be. He said if anything's easy for anyone at all, then it could be easy for anyone willing to learn the same frame of mind. Of course the actual learning could be painful, but once you've done it....

"This one's different," he merely answered.

I was tempted to give in and ask what he meant, but he never gave out his answers that easily. He always made me ask the right question, always made me figure it out for myself. He said I'd come to understand better this way. And I had to admit he was right. When I grew visibly frustrated, he'd toss out enough clues to get me moving along the right path. Our conversations were just another one of the games he played so well. This time, though, I was stumped right off the bat. I shrugged my shoulders a bit, asking for some clue as to what question I should ask to get at his real meaning.

"That's all," he answered, shrugging his shoulders back at me.

"So you're just not going to be happy?" I asked. "You're determined to be unhappy?" Ski could be stubborn, but this was ridiculous.

"I know what you're thinking," Ski said. "You're thinking it's a stupid way to live."

I nodded. It *was* stupid. I couldn't imagine why he would choose it. But I also assumed he must have solid rationalizations to support his ideas, as he always did.

"Oh, you're right, of course," he added. "It *is* stupid."

Again, I had nothing to say. I watched for his next step, his next clever move to bring the argument back onto his ground. But Ski said nothing. Perhaps he had nothing more to say. "So why don't you change?" I finally asked.

"Ha!" Ski laughed, another of his throat laughs, then shook his head. "Oh, I can't change. This one goes too deep. It's my very core. It's beyond learning—I've tried, believe me. Anyway, if I changed, I wouldn't know who I was anymore. I certainly wouldn't be *me!*"

"You can change," I argued. "You can be anything you want! If you want it bad enough...."

The Perfect Gift

"Well maybe that's it, then," he retorted sarcastically. "Maybe I just don't want it bad enough."

"So change," I repeated.

"Shut up, Spencer," he said dryly. "I don't want to talk about it."

3 One of the Family

I let it go. I wasn't much in the mood to debate now, anyway. This was supposed to be a break from studying and thinking.

I leaned back into my chair and sipped slowly at the hot chocolate. The steam rose past my eyes and clouded the world sporadically. High above campus, patches of sky cut ragged blue holes in the clouds.

Ski slumped in his chair and stared at the ground with a light frown spread across his face.

"Nice hat," I commented between sips of cocoa, changing the subject.

"This thing makes me look stupid, but what do I care? Who do I have to impress?"

"So what are you gonna do after graduation?" I asked, changing the subject again.

"Fast food. I want to put my philosophy degree to good use."

Another game. Some kind of riddle, most likely. "And how do you do that? By working at fast food or just buying a burger?"

"Working, you idiot." He shot me a quick, dirty look. "Because I'd meet a lot of people there and I could promote more sincerity in the world."

"And you would do this by...?"

"By being genuine," he answered, showing a little more energy again. "Everyone expects fast food workers to tell you to have a nice day just because you biggied your fry order. As if they care. Not me, I'd just say, 'Don't choke' or 'Hang in there.'"

"You don't mean any of this," I said, looking away. "You're just tired of finals." Ski had taken 19 credits of difficult classes and it hadn't been easy. "What are you *really* doing after graduation?"

"Fast food," he answered again. I laughed and shook my head. It was no use trying to talk today.

"Hey, you two!" Julie walked up then. She wore a red ski jacket and the faded jeans she wore on the most casual of days. Her shoulder-length blonde hair swished past her chin as she swung her backpack down from her shoulder and set it on a chair. She looked perfect, as always. "Mind if I sit?"

"Please do," Ski answered, sitting up straighter in his chair.

She leaned over and kissed me on the cheek, then sat in the chair between us. "How are my boys today?"

"Terrific," I answered. "Almost done."

"Good," she said. "What are we doing tonight?" She had a final to take in about an hour and then would be finished studying for the semester. Her last exam wasn't till early tomorrow morning, but she said she was tired of studying biology and would do just fine.

"I need to study for my French exam," I said apologetically. If I were going to squeeze an A from the class, I'd need to ace my final tomorrow. Besides, I was afraid of her guessing that I knew something that I wasn't telling her, I was afraid of somehow spoiling the surprise about the ring I hoped to give her in a few days.

"Oh, you'll do fine," she said. "Let's play! You're a natural at languages. You've got nothing to worry about."

Julie and I had taken French 1010 together last year. She was used to things coming easily to her, and when something didn't, like languages, she grew frustrated. Back then, I had an extra reason to be interested in French and it came to me naturally, but that reason had faded away.

Julie used my "brilliance," as she called it, as an excuse for us to study together. It didn't take long to recognize that she wanted more than just help with French. I remember the first time she kissed me after a late study session the night before our May final. I couldn't concentrate for the rest of the night, and she was excited when she scored higher than me the next day.

"Yeah, well I had more motivation then. It's been harder this semester."

"Is it because you don't have a study partner anymore?" she smiled. "I'm sorry, I shouldn't be so hard on you. How about if you come over and I make you dinner and help you study?"

I shook my head and laughed. "I know you better than that!" Studying would be the last thing she'd want to do.

"No, really," she insisted, "I've got some stuff I want to read, too."

"Listen," I told her, "we'll have plenty of time to play over the break."

"That's the other thing," she said, looking at me sheepishly. "After you left last night, I got thinking that this could be my last chance for a while to see my whole family together, and I already have the plane ticket and…." She stopped there, looking at me questioningly.

As the meaning of what she was saying sank in, I felt the first stabs of disappointment sink slowly into my heart. Her family all lived in Oregon, but her older brother had taken a job on the East Coast. Soon her little brothers would be moving away to college or the military and getting everyone together would never be as simple again.

"And like you say," she added, "we'll have plenty of time together after the break."

I didn't want to change our plans, but couldn't think of a reasonable argument to dissuade her without giving away my plans to ask her to marry me. I could surely come up with a Plan B. I could drive out to Oregon and visit her there, or persuade her to fly home early and then bring her to Wyoming.

"And you're making me dinner tonight, right?" I finally agreed. Maybe I could even get up enough courage to give her the ring tonight. Maybe then she would change her mind and come with me after all.

"Is that okay?" she asked, resting her hand on my knee. I took her hand and nodded yes. "Come over at six," Julie instructed. "And bring your roommate."

We both looked at Ski. He looked up and sat up a little straighter again. "No, thanks, kids. If you really wanted a third wheel, you'd get a tricycle."

Ski looked particularly lonely just then and before I thought better of it…"C'mon, Ski," I insisted, "you're one of the family."

"Family, huh? Sounds like you two are getting pretty serious!" he said. "But I have a study group tonight."

Whether or not that was the truth, we didn't press the issue. The thought of Julie and I as a family made me instantly glad Ski couldn't join us tonight. I couldn't very well propose with Ski sitting right there next to us.

"What are you doing for the break?" Julie asked him. "Since I won't be around to keep you company this year."

"Oh, I'm expecting to get a post card from my family, so I'll wait around for that." Ski's parents had already left for vacation in the Bahamas. Ski could have joined them if he wanted, but his family wasn't close and they rarely spent time together. Before he left home for college, they always bought him Christmas gifts, but now just made sure he had all the money he needed and figured that was good enough.

"You should go with Spencer!" Julie's face lit up.

Ski laughed. "Oh, sure, that's just what they need – a two-week visit from Ebenezer Scrooge."

"They'll be fine," Julie insisted. "If you don't go, I'll worry about you bored and alone here for the entire break."

He looked up at Julie, doing his best to pretend he wasn't even considering it, then glanced briefly at me.

"Come," I said. "You'll be surprised what a little home cooking will do for you." If Julie couldn't come, this would at least give me someone to talk to about her.

"If you don't go," Julie added, sensing he was beginning to sway, "I'll be forced to give you up as a friend so I won't have to worry about you, which means I'll never talk to you again."

"All right, already," he said, "I'll go. No need for threats!"

"Then it's settled," Julie said. "Good. I'll expect a full report when you get back. For now, I'm going to grab something to eat and then get another final out of the way."

"Good luck," Ski said. "And in case I don't see you again, enjoy your break!"

Julie stood up and mussed his hair through his fleece hat.

"Hey!" he protested. "You're messing up the hairdo I spent all night on!"

"Ya know what I like best about you, Ski?" Julie asked. "You always make me laugh." Ski smiled wearily at that. "Never change," Julie added. She leaned over and gave me a quick kiss on the lips. "See you tonight."

"Hey," I said as we both watched Julie walk away, "what happened to 'don't choke' or 'hang in there'? What happened to sincerity?"

"Shut up, Spencer."

I smiled victoriously. "Ya know what? A little Christmas spirit is gonna do you good."

"Bah, humbug," Ski replied.

4 Worth Waiting

Julie finished her reading half an hour ago and had been lying on the floor, doodling in her notebook while I crammed.

"Are you excited to go back to Wyoming?"

I looked down at Julie from the French textbook. "Yeah, I guess so. It's hard to think much beyond finals, though." My answer was part true and partially meant as a hint that she should be quiet and let me study.

Julie rolled over on her back and looked up at me. "I know what you mean," she said.

"You can barely think beyond the next five minutes," I pointed out.

"You're right," she answered, climbing up onto the couch next to me. "Let's live in the moment and take a study break." She pulled the highlighter from my fingers and replaced the cap.

"You can't take a break from something you haven't been doing," I pointed out, knowing all the while that resistance was futile.

Julie pulled the textbook gently from my lap and sat there herself, straddling me and wrapping her arms tightly around my neck. "Then you take a study break and I'll take a thinking break."

"What have you been thinking…" my question was cut short when her mouth covered mine. Julie was a good kisser and she knew it. She knew she could always get my attention that way. I resumed the question a minute later. "What have you been thinking about?"

"You," she answered, her arms draped around my neck, her ear pressed against mine, her teeth nibbling softly on my neck.

"And you want to take a break from thinking about me?"

"Yes."

"Why?"

"Because I keep thinking about how I won't see you after tonight for two whole weeks."

"Are you sure you don't want to come with me?" I asked.

"No. But I'm pretty sure I should spend some time with my family."

"How about flying back early? I could pick you up at the airport and take you to Wyoming for a few days."

"That sounds nice," she agreed. "What's it like there?"

"It's beautiful," I said with conviction. "The valley is mostly farmland surrounded by mountains, and it's so quiet and peaceful. The air smells so fresh and clean. Life stays simple. Going there feels like stepping back in time."

Just describing the Amber Valley made me feel nostalgic. I spent several years living there as a child and a few summers later on, and the magic had not yet entirely worn off.

"What about that girl?"

"What girl?" I asked.

"The one you were in love with last year."

That would be Annetta. I left for Wyoming last year with a major crush on Julie though I had only actually met and talked with her a day before. How could I not be crazy about her sparkling blue eyes and flashy, confident smile? She had only been interested in Ski then, so when I met Annetta on my way into the town where Grandma lived, I didn't think twice about asking her out. We went to a school play and something clicked between us almost immediately. By the time I came back to school, I thought I was in love with Netta. Who knows? Maybe I was. It didn't make any difference now.

Ski and Julie spent a lot of time together over the break, and because she wasn't his type, he talked me up so much that her interest shifted to me. Even though I had no intention of returning her sentiments, I enjoyed her company and we spent a good deal of our free time together. She loved doing everything I did, and we often went back-country skiing and spent hours talking under pale-blue winter skies. She was smart and always had plenty of interesting things to say about any subject that came up.

Perhaps nothing would have changed if I hadn't told Annetta so many stories about Julie, mostly by email after she moved to France. At first, she didn't say much about it, then she dropped hints that perhaps Julie and I spent too much time together, then she asked if I was sure that nothing was going on between us, then she began to seem distant.

Who knows, maybe that had nothing to do with Julie. Maybe that would have happened anyway. Maybe knowing each other for only two weeks before moving apart could not supply a strong enough foundation to overcome our geographical distance.

Whatever the reason, Netta and I wrote less and less often, and by April, she quit writing altogether.

Even then, I frequently saw people that reminded me of Annetta in crowds, across campus, downtown, everywhere I went. Every time, I spun back around for a double take, but of course it

The Perfect Gift

was never her. Each time, I'd get a brief flash of how it felt being close to her, holding her in my arms, staring into her bright green eyes. I tried to hold on to the feeling, but it always slipped away.

But April showers bring May flowers, and one May night after studying with Julie for our French final, we went for a walk to enjoy the spring weather. A warm rain had quit falling and breaks in the clouds showed the black, star-studded sky. We stopped at the swings at a nearby elementary school playground, and as I leaned against a swing and gazed up at the sky, Julie stepped in front of me and wrapped her arms around my neck.

We had hugged briefly before, but this time felt different. This time, Julie didn't let go. This time, I didn't either. We kissed there in the dark and didn't seem to mind when the rain began falling again.

From then on, I didn't know why Julie and I hadn't started dating months earlier. When I scanned the faces passing by in hallways and along the sidewalks between classes, I knew I'd never find anyone better than Julie. Julie was, without a doubt, one in a million. One in a billion, probably. She was smart and fun and attractive and witty and unique, and I loved her and she loved me. What more could I ask for?

With Julie always nearby, flashing her beautiful smile, standing as close to me as she could get away with, staring up at me with her bright blue eyes, touching my arm or hand at every opportunity, inching her way into my life and heart, it shouldn't have surprised me when my memories of Annetta faded completely. I still wrote now and then, but she never wrote back. I even tried calling, but she never answered.

By the end of summer when Julie returned to Utah for school, I had given up on ever hearing from Netta again. As I quit thinking about her, things with Julie got better and better. I finally wrote off Netta as a fun and interesting fling, just another random chapter in life to close and forget. Whatever her reasons for never responding, continuing to write to her when she so clearly had no interest in me would show an utter lack of self-respect.

What about Annetta now? "She's gone, Julie," I explained. "She moved to France almost a year ago. I haven't heard from her since April." I almost sounded bitter as I said it. "I have no idea what she's up to now. I'll probably never see her again. Why would you wonder about her?"

Julie pulled away from me and looked into my eyes. "I was only teasing, Spencer. Relax, okay?"

I was surprised to notice how defensive I became over the question. I must have still been a little upset at Annetta for not writing back, at least to tell me why she didn't write. We had been close enough that I at least deserved that, I thought.

But why should I care now? I had replaced her with someone even better. "Sorry," I smiled. "She just turned out to be sort of a jerk." I went to give Julie a quick kiss but she pushed back, still staring into my eyes as if trying to read something there. "What?" I asked.

"Nothing," she answered. "I used to worry about her, you know?"

"Really?" I asked. "When? Why?"

"Last spring. Because I knew you still thought about her and it made you look sad. Like you missed her a lot."

"I guess I did think about her then. But not now. I hardly even remember her."

"Good," Julie said, looking happy again. She kissed me and gave me a tight squeeze.

Midnight came and went and I finally began to drag myself home. I didn't want to leave Julie but we had grown sleepy enough that we weren't getting much out of being together anyway. I stood up, pulled on my coat and walked to the door. "Merry Christmas," I said, slipping an arm around Julie's slender waist and leaning forward for one last goodnight kiss.

"Oh yeah," she said, twisting out of my arms. "Thanks for reminding me." Julie walked back to her room and returned with a small package wrapped in metallic-green paper. "Merry Christmas," she said while handing me the gift. The box was shaped like a book but heavier. I shook it gently and it made no sound.

"Thanks!" I told her. "Should I open it now?"

"Of course not, silly! It's a Christmas gift - you have to wait till Christmas. You need something to look forward to! That's the best thing about Christmas!"

I went to hug her again, then hesitated. I had brought the ring in my coat pocket just in case the right moment arrived to give it to her tonight, but it hadn't. It had been intended as her Christmas gift but I couldn't very well use it now, not at such an ordinary moment and when we wouldn't be together to watch the diamond sparkle for at least a week.

Then again, it would be fun to send it with her to Oregon and make her open it on Christmas. I imagined her opening it in front of her whole family and the surprise they would all enjoy;

or tell her to go somewhere beautiful and open it alone. But the small, red felt box would give everything away, and she wouldn't wait, and we would get engaged in the entryway of her apartment instead of on a snowy mountaintop or in front of a warm fire in an antique house or somewhere else beautiful and memorable.

"Um," I began.

"You didn't forget my present, did you?" she asked, slipping into my arms.

"Are you kidding?" I objected. "I found you the *perfect* gift. I just can't give it to you right now."

Julie looked at me questioningly but I only answered with a raised eyebrow as if to apologize for not being able to provide any more information. "I'll give it to you when you get to Wyoming, okay? That'll give you a reason to come back as early as possible."

"A perfect gift, huh?" she asked, smiling mysteriously. "You make it sound worth waiting for."

"Believe me," I assured her. "It's very much worth waiting for. Definitely something to look forward to."

I looked into her eyes one last time, taking in a final impression, a mental picture to remember for the next week or so, a snapshot to keep fresh in my memory and to help the heart grow fonder.

A question suddenly appeared in my to mind. *Do you want Julie?* What a strange thought. Of course I did! Why wouldn't I? *Yes, I answered to myself, I do.*

Then just as suddenly, I felt an urgency to give Julie the ring. To ask her *right now* to marry me, to be my wife, and to stay with me forever. To take her in my arms and hold her as tight as I possibly could and never let her go.

The feeling came with a quickening heart beat and a tightening of my chest, turning my breath shallow. Something about the feeling seemed to tell me that it was now or never.

But it could hardly be now. This moment was too sudden. I wasn't ready. I wanted a better moment, and we would have many better moments soon enough.

There was no reason to rush. I wanted to do this right.

I stared into her blue eyes and pushed the feeling from my mind. Her stunning beauty, her confident gaze, and the love shining in her eyes reminded me why I had fallen in love with this girl in the first place.

You are worth waiting for, I thought to myself, then kissed her goodnight and walked out the door.

5 Now or Never

I stepped out into the cold night with a hot fire burning away inside my heart. I buried my face deep into the collar of my parka to protect it from the frigid air, but soon found myself tilting my head back and gazing up at the black sky, staring at the tiny, bright stabs of light floating between the clouds. I wondered which star was mine, which lucky star had made my life so sweet.

I thought quickly over the many twists and turns my life had taken. I would never understand how everything had come together and brought me to this point. But it didn't matter, I had arrived and everything felt right.

The cool night wind breathed softly from the mouth of the canyon. It felt good as the cold began to gnaw lightly on the skin of my cheeks and nose. Breaks in the fast-moving clouds showed occasional glimpses of a bright-edged moon just rising over the mountains.

I buried my hands in my pockets and walked quickly up the street toward my apartment. The air felt refreshing now but would grow uncomfortable if it found its way through the seams of my clothing.

Three blocks later as I stepped onto my front porch and turned the doorknob, something had subtly changed inside. The sweetness remained, as bright and intense as ever, but something new had made its way inside as well.

It tasted bitter and lonely. Did I miss Julie so much already? Impossible. I must have been tired and worried about finals. All the stress from the past few weeks was finally catching up to me. What else could cause such a strange feeling?

I stood on the porch for over a minute, observing this feeling, my hand still resting on the doorknob. Then I turned away from the door then and looked back up at the dark sky. I wanted to let the bitter feeling go, I wanted to walk inside feeling happy and calm, but the feeling of distress only grew stronger.

Suddenly the same question as before entered my mind. *Do you want Julie?*

Yes, I thought again, and with my answer, the same feeling I felt standing in Julie's doorway hit me like a two by four over the back of the head. *Now or never!* it shouted inside my head.

I opened the front door and set my back pack on the living room floor, then closed the door again and started running down the street into the darkness with no idea where I was going or what

I would do.

When I reached Julie's apartment, the lights were all off. She had already gone to bed.

The ring sat in my coat pocket. I took it out and opened the box, watching the diamond sparkle in the dim illumination from a nearby street light.

Perhaps right now wasn't such a bad moment after all. I could go knock on Julie's door and take her completely by surprise. It might not be as romantic as a white mountain meadow or a hearth full of glowing red coals, but those moments would come later. There would be plenty of time for everything.

Why did I feel such urgency, anyway? Most likely it was just a reaction to worrying about being left and forgotten. I had been there before and it was no fun. I didn't want to go through that again. But did I want to let a fear like that push me forward right now?

As I stood in the cold air wondering what to do, the decision seemed to be made for me. The urgency, the voice that said "Now or never!" faded slowly away until it vanished completely. In its place came a softer, duller version of the bittersweet ache.

I suddenly realized just how sweet that urgency had felt. I suddenly wanted it back with all its power and emotion. I walked quickly to Julie's door and raised my hand to knock, but stopped short. What would I say now? With no urgency pressing me forward, no joy bubbling over, this moment would no longer be right for a proposal. There would be no magic. The perfect moment had passed, so I would wait for the next one.

I turned away from the door and started running again, but not toward home. I ran partly to warm myself and partly to work the strange feeling out of my heart, letting it bounce around inside me, hoping it would shake loose and fall to the ground like so much spare change from a shallow pocket.

By the time I had run three miles and reached my front door once more, I felt tired and calm and better. The feeling had gone. I took a quick warm shower to bring the feeling back into my finger tips and face and fell asleep the moment my head hit the pillow.

6 Departure

I woke up feeling fresh and alive from last night's run. I walked to campus and took my last final, then left the building to find a warm south breeze blowing across campus. It felt good to have finished the semester.

The deep-blue sky glowed above large, puffy clouds, and I closed my eyes and turned my face upward, letting the warm rays of the sun splash over it. I exhaled and felt the cool shadows cast by the steam of my breath. A warm south breeze raised the temperatures to a comfortable forty five degrees, and I walked home with my coat only half zipped.

Of course I knew what the south wind meant. It meant that a cold front was descending from the northwest and about to collide with the warm front moving up from the south. When the fronts met, the warm, humid air from the south would cool quickly and no longer retain its moisture.

With a big cold front, huge snowflakes would fall as the storm began, and who knows how long they would continue. *I should get home and pack*, I thought, quickening my pace. But not too much, not so much that I didn't enjoy the calm walk home in this temporary spring-like warmth.

At home, I stretched out across the couch with the sunshine warming me through the living room window pane. I wanted to enjoy this bliss for a minute longer before I got busy packing. Anyway, Ski wasn't home yet, so I had time.

I awoke half an hour later when the door slammed open. "Howdy-ho!" Ski shouted through the apartment. "Let's get a-packin'!"

"Hey, Ski," I answered, waking up and blinking to clear my bleary eyes. "How'd your test go?"

"I nailed it, pardner," he answered with an exaggerated drawl. "Now giddy up, we best be gittin' off fer cowboy land!"

I hadn't seen Ski in such a good mood for a long time. A heavy course load had kept him busy, and the stress began to show early. Julie and I sometimes dragged him away from his work for a little fun, but this only seemed to make things worse. He never seemed able to forget about the work waiting for him. By October he began refusing to join us, and by November we learned not to ask.

"I say, pardner," Ski said thoughtfully, "whose hos' we gonna ride off to the lone prairie?"

The Perfect Gift

"I'll drive," I answered, putting my feet on the floor and stretching.

Ski walked back to his room and returned with two packed duffel bags. "Let's go," he said. "We're burnin' daylight."

"I still have to pack," I said.

"What's the matter with you, son?" Ski asked. "You've had plenty o' time ta git ready."

"Well I didn't know you were packed," I said. "And when I got home and you weren't here yet…what took you so long, anyway?" Our finals started at the same time and Ski usually finished tests quickly.

"I got there late and was the last one finished."

Now I understood. Ski had left home early to study, then studied half way through the test time until he was ready. Good thinking. No wonder he was so happy. I should have thought to do that with my French test.

I packed in fifteen minutes and Ski helped me carry my bags outside to the car. "'Bout time," he complained. "Now let's hit the road."

"Hey, Spencer, how does it feel to be finished?" Ben asked cheerfully. Ben was our neighbor and my last-year roommate, extremely talkative, and astonishingly self-centered. Not that he was self*fish*, but his thoughts never strayed far from his own person. A conversation with him could delay our departure by an unpleasant half-hour.

"It hasn't sunk in just yet," I answered, "but I'm sure it will soon enough." I opened my car trunk and dropped my bags inside.

"How'd you do on your tests?" he asked, trying again to start up a conversation.

"I'll let you know in January," I answered, trying to evade Ben's persistence.

"He's had a rough week," said Ski. I felt the corners of my mouth begin to turn up. Ski was about to make up some humorous lie. Whatever it was, he'd expect me to play along. "He asked Julie to marry him last night."

"Ski, you promised you wouldn't tell anyone," I whined.

"Wow!" Ben sounded surprised. "Congratulations!"

"Thanks," I answered casually.

"Only problem," Ski added, "is that she hasn't answered him. She said she needs the break to think it over. Now Spencer's convinced he has to find her the perfect gift to sway her decision."

"Hmm." Ben didn't know what to say to that. "Have you

thought about a stuffed animal or a plant?"

We both just stared at him in mild astonishment.

"And Ski, does this mean you might need a new roommate?" Ben asked hopefully. I wondered why Ben would continually seek our company when we never treated him with a whole lot of respect – especially Ski. It must have something to do with wanting respect from people who he respected, since he didn't give most people the time of day.

"We're gonna have to wait till next month to start talking about that one," Ski answered.

"We'd better get shopping," I said. "I'd never forgive myself if the perfect gift sold out right before we got there."

"Yeah, good luck!" Ben added enthusiastically. I wondered how much of his excitement was for Julie and I and how much came from the possibility of rooming with Ski.

"Thanks," I answered. "See ya after the break."

"That's funny you should say all that about the perfect gift for Julie," I told Ski once we had the car rolling out of the parking lot. "'Cause last night we were talking and…"

"Oh, I know all about that," Ski said. "You told her you got her the perfect gift only you couldn't give it to her yet."

"How d'you know about all that?" I asked, surprised.

"She told me."

"When?"

"This morning."

"When this morning?" I persisted. Ski's and Julie's finals almost overlapped. They must have run into each other on campus. I felt a little jealous, or rather, I missed Julie and regretted not meeting her just for a minute before she flew home.

"At breakfast."

"Oh, did you run into her at the Student Center?" I asked.

"No," Ski answered, looking out his window. "I took her out to breakfast to apologize for spending so little time with you guys this semester."

I wished he'd have invited me, but at the same time understood why he didn't. He'd have been the third wheel then and wouldn't be very comfortable if we got even the least bit mushy. I couldn't blame him for wanting a few moments alone with her, though I still felt a little envious.

"How did you have time for that?" I asked. With their finals overlapping….

"That's why I was late for my final, Sherlock. She finished

hers after only an hour and I got to mine an hour late, so we had two full hours. That's the problem with you English majors—no basic math skills."

"Yeah, yeah," I said. "Anyway, that's cool you got to see her." Again I wished I could have seen her once more, could have said goodbye one more time. I wished that *I* were leaving town first so I could stop by her place on my way out of town. It would be better now, I would feel more relaxed with no more finals to study for, with nothing left to worry about.

After a brief silence with the radio playing, Ski spoke again. "Now don't you be jealous, young whipper snapper, but she gave me a great big hug and even kissed me on the cheek."

"Did she mention anything about sending one for me?"

"Even if she had," Ski answered, "You could forget it! There's no way I'm delivering any hugs or kisses in your direction!"

7 'Tis the Season

We took the long way to Wyoming. Going through Salt Lake would add an hour or two to the trip but would also give me a chance to do some gift shopping. Besides, neither of us knew exactly when the storm would hit. Staying on major highways would be safer than taking our chances through obscure mountain pass shortcuts.

We parked at the mall and walked inside a department store, where the bright lights and colorful holiday decorations contrasted sharply with the dreary gray clouds that covered the sky outside. As I had hoped, the store had many last-minute sale signs. That would save my meager student budget, especially considering my upcoming ring payments. It felt good to have finals over, to finally be able to relax and enjoy the Christmas spirit.

"Don't ya just hate Christmas?" Ski mused.

"How can you hate Christmas?" Nothing Ski said surprised me anymore.

"Just look around!" he said, waving an arm toward the decorations. "Doesn't this disturb you?"

I looked around but only found holiday colors, bright lights, and cheerful music playing softly. I shrugged my shoulders. "What?"

"It's all so shallow, don't ya think?" Ski looked genuinely

frustrated. "I mean, what's Christmas supposed to be about?"

"Peace. Hope. Love," I answered.

"Exactly!" Ski accentuated the word by stabbing a finger into the air. "It's supposed to be about love, so then everyone goes out and buys *things* for each other. As if that's all love is. It reminds me of an abusive relationship where the perpetrator goes and buys gifts as if that could make up for the abuse. It's downright depressing."

"Sounds a lot like *your* parents," I pointed out.

"Exactly," Ski agreed. "That's the kind of thing I'm talking about."

"But not everyone's like your parents, and gifts are only part of the season," I argued. "You can't call someone abusive just because they gave you something."

"Yeah," Ski admitted, "but it makes it so easy to be shallow, to not really develop deeper feelings for anyone."

"You're one to talk," I accused. Ski was acting unreasonable and uncharacteristically negative. I thought it absurd that he would be so determined to see only his side of this issue. "After all, how many people do *you* really care about? I can only think of two."

"Yeah, that's true," Ski admitted. Rather than getting defensive at this point as I expected him to, he softened. He looked at me and smiled a weary smile. He looked tired and defeated, but there seemed to be a touch of calmness at the same time.

I felt certain that he knew that I had referred to myself and Julie as the two people he cared about, and perhaps the confession that I knew it, that I knew we were true friends, that he could really count on me, and that I genuinely cared, perhaps that meant something to him. He punched me lightly on the shoulder.

"And even with Julie and me," I thought out loud, "you don't really go out of your way to spread any cheer. You're just lucky we both like you so much!"

"Also true," he admitted again, raising one eyebrow, and we walked on in silence.

I looked into the storefronts as we walked by, hoping something would catch my attention. We walked past a store filled with all kinds of clothing and trinkets. I wandered inside and up and down the aisles. Nothing really caught my eye, but I didn't even know where to begin.

"Can I help you find something?"

I looked up at the salesgirl. I was about to give her the old 'I was just looking' line, but her face caught my eye and I hesitated. Maybe she could help. She had shiny dark hair and beautiful dark eyes but they looked tired, like she had been working all day long. Her name tag said Mindy. "Yeah," I answered. "Maybe."

"What sort of thing are you looking for?" she asked.

"Well that's the problem," I told her. "I don't really know." I wanted to get a little gift for Julie in case Christmas arrived before the perfect moment to give her the ring. "I want something nice, but something with meaning, ya know? And not something too normal, either. Something maybe a little uncommon to make it special. Am I making any sense? I don't even know how to explain what I want."

Mindy smiled at my frustration. "That's a tough one, all right," she admitted. A bit of the tiredness seemed to be wearing off and her eyes brightened a bit.

"Let me just ask it this way," I said, hoping she could get me started in the right direction. "What would a beautiful girl like you want for Christmas?" Her eyes brightened a little more and she smiled again. "After all," I added, "you must have some good ideas, working in the mall and all."

"The truth is," she answered, playfully now, "I'd love anything from a good looking guy like you, as long as it comes with dinner."

I hadn't meant to sound like I was hitting on Mindy, but no harm done. "So suppose I got something for her and gave it to her over dinner. What would be a good something?"

"Depends," Mindy answered. "How much are you planning to spend on this girl? How well do you know her?"

"Pretty well. Maybe something around twenty-five dollars, or fifty if it's exceptional. I'm still a poor student with some big bills coming up, but it's more important that it's a perfect gift."

"Perfect, huh?" Mindy thought about that for a moment. "In that case, price doesn't matter. You just need something with a special meaning."

"Oh, yeah? Like what?" Mindy was the right girl to ask, alright. She seemed to know exactly what I meant.

"Anything that shows that you're really thinking of her. Something to remind her of where you met or your first date or your first kiss." I watched Mindy's dark eyes as she spoke and realized that she was watching mine as well, watching for clues about the girl I was shopping for, wondering how serious we might be and gauging the chances of me asking her out. The attention felt flattering but of course I wasn't interested.

"You're smart," I told her. "That gives me something to think about."

"What if it's just for a best friend?" Ski had wandered up behind me.

"Same thing," Mindy answered. "If it's a real friend, she'll only care that you care and you're thinking of her."

As Ski and Mindy continued talking, I wandered the aisles again. I picked up a tiny paperweight of the Eiffel Tower. That might remind her of our French class, but it also reminded me of Annetta. I'd buy it just in case and hope to find something better later on. I finally made my way to the register and Mindy walked over to ring up the sale.

"Merry Christmas," she said, smiling as she handed me the receipt. "And you, Madison," she said, turning to Ski and reaching out to touch his sleeve, "you be careful up there!"

"What was that all about?" I asked Ski once we left the store.

"Oh, I told her that your grandmother's roof collapsed under all the snow and you brought me along to climb the roof and tie a safety line to the chimney."

"What for?"

Ski usually created his little stories for people he didn't like or respect, just to have a little sport at their expense, and he had seemed to like Mindy. "So we won't fall off the roof."

Ski knew what I really meant to ask. He was being either playful or evasive. "No, I mean why did you tell her all that?"

"She's been working sixty hours a week since most of her coworkers went home for the break. So she's a little tired of Christmas and I thought a little story of Christmas in action might inspire her."

"Looks like it worked," I said, remembering how much happier she looked as we left. "But what's up with this sudden change? You haven't been seeing ghosts of Christmas past and future, have you?"

"Nope, I'm just going out of my way to spread a bit of cheer. Thought I'd give it a try. No reason."

"And why'd you let her call you Madison?"

"You ask too many questions," Ski merely answered. "Listen, I'm tired of shopping. How long are you gonna take?"

"Not too long," I answered. "I just have to find something for my little sisters."

"Then I'm going across the street to check out the lights at Temple Square. When should I meet you?"

"How about half an hour?" I asked. "I'll find you at the south gates."

The Perfect Gift

"Good enough. See you then."

Ski wandered away and disappeared in the crowd. I turned the opposite direction and went back to wandering past store fronts, hoping something would catch my eye.

8 The Tangled Web

After picking up a few more gifts, I made my way out the mall's north entrance and crossed the street. I found Ski sitting on the cement sidewalk next to a vagrant man holding a large tin can and a cardboard sign that read "Santa Claus is watching."

The man's thin but tall frame and the few deep wrinkles criss-crossing his face made him look about sixty years old. His coat showed some stains but appeared warm enough. His patent-leather shoes looked worn but functional. I wondered if he bought them at the Salvation Army store a few blocks away.

His old hat stood out as his most memorable piece of clothing. The leather cap had some sort of insignia embossed above a short visor, and would have made the man look sharp and handsome despite the wear if he had shaved more recently.

A woman dressed in a gray wool skirt and a purple ski parka stepped in front of me and leaned over to drop a few coins in the man's can.

"God bless you, ma'am," said the man, looking up into her face as she turned away. Ski looked up, too, and saw me leaning against the wall.

"Hey, Spencer!" Ski held out his hand for me to pull him up from the sidewalk. He stretched his legs while he continued talking. "Rod, this is the guy I was just tellin' you about."

I smelled trouble immediately, but kept smiling as I extended my hand to shake the man's.

"Spencer, meet Rod. Rod, Spence. Rod used to work on a horse ranch down in California."

"Sounds great. Nice to meet you, Rod."

"Likewise. Spare some change?"

"Sure." I pulled off a glove, reached into a pocket, and tossed a few coins and a dollar into his can.

"I think it's great," Rod said, "what you're doing with your dude ranch."

"Well," I answered, wondering what Ski had told him, "it seemed like a good thing to do."

"I'll say!" Rod said enthusiastically, his entire face lighting up. "Those poor children. You must be losing an awful lot of money on this."

"Well, I've always thought money's a bit overrated anyway." I hoped I wouldn't say anything contrary to Ski's story—that was the unspoken contest Ski often dragged me into—whether I would catch on quickly enough to not get caught.

"Besides," Ski said, "we're expecting donations to start coming in soon." A few snowflakes began falling as we talked.

"We should probably be on our way," I said, sensing an out, "before the storm hits."

"Hey, Rod," Ski jumped in, "is your hat for sale? I'll give you a hundred bucks for it."

"Well, this hat has gone a lot o' places with me, but fer a hundred bucks, you got yerself a deal. Should suit your part in the play jus' right, too."

Ski the actor, I thought; *that* part of Ski's story is no lie.

"Great! Sure appreciate it, Rod. And here, I won't be needing this one anymore." Ski pulled off his fleece hat and handed it to Rod, along with five twenty-dollar bills. "It ought to keep you warm, though."

"Well I surely do appreciate it, Madison."

I was surprised again. Only Ski's mother called him by his first name anymore, and now he had told it to two total strangers in a row. We said goodbye, then walked to the curb and stopped, waiting for the signal to change to cross the street.

"It *was* thoughtful of you to host all the kids when the boys' ranch burned down, ya know," Ski said.

"You seem to be enjoying your new way of spreading holiday cheer," I pointed out. The 'walk' light lit up and we stepped into the street.

"Oh, and Mr. Jamison?" Rod called out behind us.

"That's you," Ski whispered quickly. I turned back toward Rod.

"I was sorry to hear about your wife."

I paused for a moment. "Thank you," I said sincerely, "and Merry Christmas."

We turned away again and I raised an inquisitive eyebrow toward Ski.

"Pneumonia," he replied. "There was nothing the doctors could do."

9 Over the River and Through the Woods

Inside the mall parking terrace, I threw the car keys to Ski after unlocking the doors. I had stayed up a little too late last night, so Ski would take the first driving shift while I slept. He opened his door and climbed in behind the wheel.

"I think Rod really likes you, Ski."

"Why wouldn't he?"

"And that was nice of you to buy his hat."

"I happen to like this hat! You can't buy 'em in stores all worn in like this! It's from the ranch he used to work at. He was the one doing *me* a favor." Ski held the hat out in front of me to examine, but didn't put it on. It would need washing first.

"Still," I said, "a hundred dollars…."

"I've been saving up for years," Ski explained, "by never buying any gifts. I invest everything in a mutual fund. It's doing quite well."

We drove out of the terrace and headed toward the highway through swirling snowflakes. I had a few shopping bags on the floor by my feet and lifted all but the smallest into the back seat. From it I took the miniature Eiffel Tower and held it up to examine.

"Who's that for?" Ski asked, glancing at the trinket.

"I don't know," I answered blandly.

"You just bought it for no one?" Ski seemed to think I was hiding something. "Are you sure it's not for someone who speaks a little French, someone you love very much?"

"I thought I could decide who to give it to later," I said. "Maybe I'll give it to you since you seem so fascinated by it."

"You mean [*sniff, sniff*] you would give something so precious [*sniff*] to *me?*"

Ski's sarcasm deserved no answer. Instead, I set the tower below the radio and changed the subject. "Hey, why did you let Rod and Mindy call you Madison?"

Now came Ski's turn to ignore me. He just reached down and turned up the radio, and any further conversation got buried by the music.

Ski drove through town a little faster than I felt comfortable with, but I didn't want to say anything, which would only encourage him to drive even faster, so I leaned my seat back and closed my eyes, ready for some sleep before my turn to drive came in a few hours. I felt the car accelerate and looked up through the windshield just in time to see a red light sail by overhead. Ski laughed once and started singing along with the music.

I closed my eyes again and let the sounds of the music, the engine, and Ski's singing blend together and eventually disappear in the distance, in the empty space between reality and silent dreams of white Wyoming snow and tall, snow-covered pine trees:

In my dream, I walk through wide fields of freshly fallen snow, lifting my feet high with each step through the deep powder.

The sky has cleared and snowflakes strewn across the landscape sparkle brightly in the moonlight.

Tree branches sag under the weight of the heavy snowfall and each branch blends into the next, making the pines look like thick, ornate candles that have burned and melted for hours before being snuffed out.

Stars shine brightly above the field—more stars than I remember seeing for a long, long time.

I suddenly notice the voices of a choir surging over the landscape. Powerful and beautiful harmonies overwhelm me as they gently fill the dark night sky with a glorious harmony from horizon to horizon.

The choir sings songs I've never heard before, and I don't understand the words. I only know that they mean True Love, Pure Joy, Deep Peace, and Enduring Hope.

I look up, expecting to see angels filling the sky, the heavenly host proclaiming joy to the world, good will toward men; but only the bright, tiny stars in the black midnight sky stare back down at me.

My six-year old sister Diane walks up next to me and takes my hand. I point to the stars and ask if she hears them singing, too. She does and we stand together in the snow and listen.

Diane starts to sing along and I'm amazed that she knows the words as I listen to the sweet voice I didn't know she possessed. My youngest sister suddenly seems centuries older and wiser than me. I feel young and foolish and lost in comparison.

"Hey, Spencer—you wanna drive?" Ski woke me just as Diane had looked up into my eyes, about to tell me the secret to everything I ever wanted to know.

The Perfect Gift

10 Home for the Holidays

Two hours later, Ski and I pulled off the highway in Amber, Wyoming. The storm had passed after dumping a foot and a half of powder on the world, and a full moon shone on miles of soft, inviting snow fields. The roads hadn't been cleared recently, but a few vehicles had passed by, digging deep enough grooves in the snow that I didn't worry about getting stuck.

As always, it felt good to arrive. Even though years had passed since I spent more than a few weeks at a time here, Amber held enough childhood memories that Grandma's house would always feel like home, and the sensation of magic wonder would always linger, perhaps because I hadn't stayed around long enough since then to wear out the feeling.

As we drove past the dark shape of the diner where Annetta and her sister Amy worked last year, different feelings swept through me. Warm, bittersweet memories of the exciting infatuation that Netta made me feel, followed immediately by a hint of the disappointment that followed when she stopped writing.

I let the pointless thoughts about Netta drift away and be forgotten. If I thought about her too much, I'd just get mad again that she hadn't even had the consideration to write and tell me why she stopped writing.

At Grandma's home, we pulled in through the log fence lining the property. Ski stirred in the passenger seat and woke up as the car came to a stop in the circular driveway. He sat up and stared at the house as I shut off the engine.

"Gosh, Little Joe," he said groggily, "sure feels good to be back at the Ponderosa."

I knew what he meant. Except for the snow and the three-story house, something about the antique architecture of Grandma's place and the way it stood alone between pines and cottonwoods in the middle of nowhere reminded me of the ranch house on the old western series *Bonanza*.

Warm, yellow light flowed like honey onto the snow through small windows in the spiral staircase at the center of the house. The peaked roof easily shed snow, saving the house from the danger of buildup and collapse.

The cold bit instantly at our noses and throats as we opened the car doors and carried our bags inside. Snow crunched and squeaked like a dull musical instrument beneath our feet, but we both felt too tired to appreciate the song.

The front door was unlocked, as always. It seemed strange, after having lived away from the country for so long, to be so careless. At the same time, it felt refreshing. Refreshing to return to a place where theft rarely happened, and it created a warm, homey feeling, because I knew I was always welcome and didn't even have to knock.

We dropped our bags inside near the front door and made our way toward the wood burning stove in the living room. The sounds of wood popping and fizzing inside added to the magic of this frontier-style home. The house had twelve bedrooms, and each would soon fill with guests. Ski and I would stay in my old room, and kids would sack out on couches and the floor upstairs, next to another wood burning stove that would warm them all night long, as long as somebody remembered to wake up once or twice and toss in more logs.

We had approached the living room stove and held out our hands toward its steady heat when someone stirred on the couch behind us.

"Ahh, you're here, Spencer," Grandma said. "I'm so glad. I worried that the storm might delay you." She must have tried to wait up, I thought as I glanced her way.

"It wasn't bad, really. There was just enough traffic to keep the snow from piling up deep."

Grandma had been sitting on the couch wrapped in a patchwork quilt. She stood up and I gave her a hug as she kissed my cheek. Her gray hair was pulled back in a pony tail, and her thin frame looked sturdy and strong beneath the heavy blanket draped around her shoulders.

On the mantle behind her sat a photo of her with Grandpa taken two and a half years ago, just before he suffered a heart attack and passed away in his sleep.

Grandma was one of my favorite people. Wise without being preachy, kind yet direct, genuine and generous and loving.

"And this is my roommate Ski," I said.

"I'm glad you could come with Spencer, Ski, and I hope you'll feel perfectly comfortable here."

"Thanks," Ski answered, still groggy. He moved nearer to the stove, still holding his hands out toward the warmth, and closed his eyes. I doubted that he'd remember the introduction in the morning.

Out of the corner of my eye, I saw Ski swaying back and forth slowly, catching himself just before he actually tipped over.

"Looks like I'd better show Ski to our room," I said, "before he falls asleep standing up."

"Get some sleep yourself. We'll have plenty of time to talk tomorrow."

After showing Ski to our room, I walked back downstairs to the computer, turned it on and sent Julie a quick e-mail.

Hey Julie,
How was your trip? Ski and I just arrived, safe and sound. Good thing, too—I'm about to fall asleep sitting here at the computer.
Have you thought about when you want to fly back? You will love it here for sure! The snow is so beautiful. Let me know—I'm already dying to see you!
Love you tons!
Spence

Normally, I would have called or texted or instant messaged, but Amber had no cell service, and my parents, aunts and uncles had purposefully set up a satellite internet connection that only connected to this computer with no wireless available for my phone.

The phone wires were so old that they only supported the town party line, which I opted not to use since half a dozen strangers would certainly be listening in on whatever we said.

Upstairs, I changed into my pajamas, jumped into bed beneath heavy quilts and fell asleep as soon as the bed warmed up, the last sounds to register on my senses being the crackles and pops in the stove downstairs and Ski's light snores from the bed near the window.

11 Suffer the Children

I awoke late the next morning to warm sunlight pouring in from outside and the noise of activity that had probably rumbled downstairs for an hour or two already. Ski was already awake and lay on his stomach staring out the window.

"Well, it *is* as beautiful as you said, I have to give it that."

I sat up and slid my feet onto the floor. Stepping over to the window, I found that last night's storm had left the familiar scene even more stunning than I remembered. Thirty feet from the house, tall pines grew toward the sky, their strong branches bending dangerously beneath a heavy load of new powder.

Above the trees, bright sunshine reflected from smooth, rolling mountains and I had to look away, my eyes not yet accustomed to the light.

Just then, my sister walked past in the hall and peered in through the cracked door. "Spencer's awake!" The door was thrust open and Diane burst in, jumping up for me to catch her in my arms and swing her around.

"Hey, kid, good to see ya! How've you been? You look terrific!"

Diane laughed and shrieked as I swung her in circles around the room. In the middle of one spin, I caught a glimpse of Ski smiling, but he had regained his composure by the time we stopped spinning and Alisha ran in for her bear hug. Ski had seen the letters and "I love you" finger paintings I received at school and knew how my sisters and I adored each other.

Finally, we stopped and sat on the edge of Ski's bed. Alisha sat next to me and I put my arm around her shoulders.

"This is my friend Ski who I told you about."

"All good, I'm sure," added Ski.

"Is Ski your real name?" asked Diane. "'Cause Alisha says it can't be your real name. She says you made it up."

As Ski smiled at the little girl's boldness, I answered for him. "Yep, Ski's his real name, but it's really his middle name. His first name's Madison, but he says if you call him that," my voice dropped to a whisper with plenty of tease in it, "he'll deck ya!" This was Ski's traditional answer to the common question, but I wasn't sure if he'd have the guts to threaten my little sisters.

"Well, it's a cool name," added Di. "It's a lot better than 'Diane.'"

"No way!" Ski responded. "Do you know how to say 'Diane' in Spanish? 'Diana.' It means 'bull's-eye' or the trumpet call when an army charges. I think Diane's a pretty cool name."

Diane smiled animatedly and her eyes gleamed. "Oh."

"Wanna know how I got my name?" Ski asked.

"Yeah, sure," answered Diane, her eyes widening, ready for a story.

"Well, I had this lunatic uncle, see," Ski's eyes rose momentarily, focusing on nothing, waiting for the story to fall into place in his mind. "And he used to play all kinds of practical jokes and take stupid dares. He was the biggest show off in town, and he'd do anything for attention. They called him Crazy Larry. Well, he and my dad grew up in Alaska, and they'd go skiing almost every day after school.

"During the Spring of their junior year, a new girl moved into town. Her name was Angela. She had long, brown hair, dark eyes, and all the guys in school were totally knocked out by her. Crazy Larry, of course, was desperate to impress her first. So desperate, in fact, that he started getting on everyone's nerves.

"One day, everybody was crowding around Angela in the school cafeteria and Larry was really shooting off his mouth. Well, it just so happens that there was this cliff that dropped into a lake near town. There was an old legend about somebody skiing off the cliff into the lake and getting frozen under the ice and haunting the place ever since. Well the ice had just thawed for the Spring and my dad walked up to Crazy Larry and dared him to ski off the cliff.

"I don't think Dad really expected Larry to accept the dare, but it obviously scared Larry. He was about to laugh it off, but suddenly, out of the corner of his eye, he noticed that Angela was now looking straight at him and waiting for his answer! As all the guys followed her gaze, everyone grew quiet.

"Larry desperately wanted to say no, but it was too much against his nature. He just grinned and said, 'Sure, I'll do it.' With the words spoken, there was no going back.

"Then the fear faded just enough to allow Crazy Larry's brain to start working again, and he added, '*if* you name your first son *Madison*.' It was a last-ditch effort to get out of the whole thing.

"Angela's jaw dropped. All the guys gasped. 'How could anyone agree to name their son *Madison*?' they whispered among themselves. 'How could anyone be so cruel?'

"But now the pressure fell on Dad. He folded and agreed to the deal. That afternoon, with the whole school watching, and Angela looking more stunning than ever, Crazy Larry skied off the cliff and into the lake below and was never seen again, except on the eve of Dad's and Angela's wedding, when many people reported seeing a dripping-wet boy in ski boots walking around the old high school repeating, 'You promised to name him Madison! You promised me! You promised!'

"Pretty weird, huh?"

"Yeah," answered Diane, her eyes wider than before. Alisha looked at me with a dubious expression and shook her head. I smiled and her mouth broke into a grin.

"I hate that story," Ski sighed. "My dad used to tell it every time I brought a date home."

"So how come they named you Madison *Ski*?" Diane asked.

"Oh, that part's even weirder. See, Angela had this cousin...."

"Everybody come downstairs for breakfast!"

Just as the voice called us down, the warm smells of hash browns, bacon, scrambled eggs, juice, whole milk, muffins and butter, and pancakes dripping with maple syrup rose up the stairwell. Ski's story would have to wait. He looked at me and rolled his eyes, this time as if to say, "Your little sister's a real dope," but I could tell he liked her.

We found our places around the two large tables in the dining room while everyone hugged me or patted me on the shoulder and shook my hand. I introduced Ski all around and he smiled, nodded, and said hello politely.

Grandma told him good morning and asked how the trip out was. I watched Ski almost wince at the 'good morning'—one of those phrases he didn't believe in—then an eyebrow raised as he considered the possibility that this actually *was* a good morning.

"The drive was fine," he answered, "except for Spencer's driving. He was so excited to get here, he nearly got us killed leaving Salt Lake City. Somebody ought to tell him to slow down."

"Yes, Spencer," my grandmother smiled, "we'd have saved you some food even if you arrived late."

There was no use fighting back, no use pointing out that Ski had been the one running red lights out of the city. I just smiled and nodded at Grandma and launched into the golden-brown buttermilk pancakes.

Soon the plates of food had stopped passing and the family had settled into various conversations. We learned that Jared and Cassie, the last of the cousins, had been stopped by last night's storm and would arrive in the afternoon. I sat back and listened to everyone talk while sipping my juice slowly. Ski also listened and helped himself to the last strip of bacon.

"Good stuff, huh?" I asked.

"Whoa!" he answered. "I just passed up my RDA of fat for the whole week." I appreciated the fact that he only whispered the comment to me under his breath.

Breakfast finished up and people began to pick up their dishes and carry them to the kitchen sink.

"All you guys go play some games, I'll take care of the dishes," Grandma said.

"No, mom," my dad cut in, "you cooked. Let us guys do the

The Perfect Gift

dishes."

"No, no, no," Grandma protested. Dad and Uncle Jon prevailed and everyone else wandered upstairs to shower and dress for the day.

"Spence, you should have warned me we'd be spending the holidays at the Beaver Cleaver residence." He looked smug and condescending, as if everyone's politeness was naive and he knew something they didn't. An argument on the subject didn't interest me, so I just ignored him.

After finishing the dishes, Ski yawned. "I'm gonna go get better acquainted with the furniture," he said as he wandered toward the living room for a nap.

I poured myself another glass of juice, then headed for the living room to read. Diane had walked in a few steps before me and stepped around the couch where Ski sat facing away from the door. She picked up the Bible and sat down next to him.

"Hi, kid."

"Read me the Christmas story, Ski. It's right here."

Someone had left the red thread marker in Luke chapter two. Ski looked down into her bright blue eyes and hesitated momentarily. He wasn't religious and always either joked about the subject or avoided it entirely.

"Lemme see that thing," he conceded, giving in to her expectant eyes.

"Thanks!"

I quickly and quietly turned and left the room. As I made my way toward the stairs, I heard Ski's voice reading, "And it came to pass in those days, that there went out a decree from Caesar Augustus, that all the world should fork over their hard-earned dough...."

In my room, I pulled wool socks, gloves, my ski parka, and pant shell from a suitcase and headed back downstairs. As I walked past the living room door again, Ski's improvisation was in full swing.

"And she brought forth her first-born son, and wrapped him in swaddling clothes, and laid him in a manger; because there was no room for them in the Motel 5. It was a real dive, but Joe was desperate. The owner just shook his head and said, 'No way, man, there's no room! The fire marshal's already on my case for over-crowding this joint! I could lose my business license!'"

Diane's laughter filled in the spaces between Ski's words as I walked to the back door, where I found my old cross-country skis and boots. Too much fresh snow had fallen to let go to waste. I pulled on the boots and warm clothing, and soon found myself stepping and gliding smoothly along the snow-covered dirt road toward the hills.

12 The Magic Forest

I had forgotten how deep my love ran for the vacant hills and rolling canyon walls north of Grandma's home where I had played endlessly as a child. The silence and space seemed to stretch on forever.

I skied forward and upward, following a gradual ridge to the first plateau. It stretched out for a quarter mile before rising into the next range of hills. Despite the cold air, the exertion of skiing warmed me completely. I unzipped my jacket and continued onward.

In every direction, I found the same familiar horizon I enjoyed as a child. Other than the sparse trees – stunted, twisted junipers with their pale blue-green berries – and an occasional bluff or wooded ravine, the landscape lay entirely empty. This world had remained completely unchanged since I roamed it as a child. All the memories of my youth came rushing back like a flash flood. I felt the boy I once was stir inside me.

The memory of my boyish outlook felt simple and happy. Life back then consisted of a few chores and endless exploration. I rarely thought of the future, and when I did, my vision rarely stretched beyond the next few days or weeks.

Years ago, I grew up and left that world behind. I forgot the simplicity that had served as my only perspective. I took on responsibilities and learned that living takes work and isn't always easy. I suffered minor disappointments and losses and put up thin walls to protect my heart from suffering the consequences.

I no longer saw the world purely as something to explore and enjoy. Now I viewed it mostly as something to survive and endure, enjoying the rewards only after working to earn them. I was happy enough, but it felt different than the simple, easy joy of childhood. Joy was out there, but now came in rare spurts rather than one never-ending stream.

But here in the winter afternoon stillness, I began to forget about all the struggle and to live only in the moment. And no wonder! I had no pressing duties or concerns to return to for weeks and I could afford to forget them for a while. I smiled wide and sucked in a deep lung-full of cold, dry, clean air.

The old mystery returned. Life felt magical. Imagination ruled. Anything could happen, anything was possible. In the canyons below, winding down from the plateau to the valley floor, the enchanted forest loomed and invited me to enter.

I skied along the plateau for half a mile before choosing a random ravine to explore. My skis clattered across wind-crusted snow as I skied over the brink and down toward the pine forest. The trees began and I stepped and slid through knee-deep powder in the wind-protected glade.

A few minutes later, I entered a clearing and glided to a stop near the center. Tall pines guarded the quiet meadow. Something about the place seemed vaguely familiar, and I searched my boyhood memories for something that happened in a place like this, but found nothing.

Just as I began to ski forward again, a log half buried in the center of the clearing caught my attention.

I suddenly knew where I stood. This was the clearing where Annetta and I had built a fire last New Year's Eve and stayed up till dawn, watching the embers sink slowly deeper through the snow.

I glanced up at the pale sky and remembered the falling stars that had streaked by overhead. I glanced down at the clearing again and suddenly felt alone. An eerie feeling washed over me and the skin on the nape of my neck crawled. I had the distinct impression that someone was watching me.

I felt an urge to look behind me, and I peered through the trees, searching the shadows for movement, but saw nothing. I held my breath and listened, but heard only my own heart beating quickly in my ears.

Suddenly a face appeared before me. It was only my imagination, but the intense green eyes startled me anyway.

The face was Annetta's. Her expression was nothing like the one she wore in this clearing a year ago. It wasn't warm and open, not in love and happy. Instead, she looked cold and direct, intense and burning.

She was like that, wasn't she? Always something burning away inside. I had forgotten. I had pushed away all memories of her, forgotten all I could, and all for the best. There was no good reason to remember her now.

I imagined her staring at me for several seconds, looking

through me, reading my heart and mind, and then she was gone and I stood alone again in the clearing.

The enchanting feeling of the forest had been replaced with a haunting aura. The face had seemed so real! As if this memory had been waiting for me here, all this time, just waiting to jump out and surprise me. Almost as if Netta had stepped out from behind a tree without me noticing, though the nearest tree stood twenty feet away.

It felt spooky to stand here alone in the stillness with my skin crawling, but just like every thriller movie ever made, something about the haunting left me feeling curious, wanting to stick around and experience the haunting again, if necessary, just to solve the mystery.

This is the part of the movie where the audience shouts "Run! Run away, you fool!" but of course the protagonist never does. He sticks around to satisfy his curiosity and ends up dead or narrowly escapes some other terrible fate.

The eeriness continued and I finally decided to leave. I suddenly wanted to get away from the clearing as quickly as possible. I could solve the mystery later, if at all!

Even as I skied away through the trees, watching the shadows closely, my heart pounding rapidly, I still felt the feeling tugging at me inside, pulling me back to explore and discover. I still felt the uncomfortable sensation like Netta was hovering just behind me, watching me go, her eyes boring holes into my back.

13 Epiphany

I skied home hot and ready for a warm shower. Ski caught me on my way upstairs.

"Hey," He said, looking distressed, "what are you doing leaving me here alone? It's hard enough pretending to be polite when I don't have to talk, but everybody keeps asking me personal questions like they're doing some kind of special report!"

"You've never been one to avoid conversation, Ski," I noted. "Why the sudden aversion?" I started walking upstairs toward our room and Ski followed.

"I don't know, man, that's what bothers me!"

I walked into the room and tossed my coat on the bed while Ski continued.

"I know I've always got plenty of smart-aleky things to say, but here, it's like those things just don't fit. So all of a sudden, I'm speechless. And it's driving me crazy!"

I just looked at him. "Talking's always a game for you. Is there some reason you don't want to play with my family?"

"Yeah, maybe that's it—it's like I'm afraid of getting sarcastic and hurting someone's feelings and things turning awkward."

"Since when do you care about hurting somebody's feelings?" I asked.

"Since I'm stuck here for two more weeks, that's when!"

"Is it impossible for you to be nice for two weeks?" I asked. "Like with Mindy and Rod last night?"

"Oh, sure," Ski answered, "we could play a two-week game of deception. Brilliant idea. That would be really relaxing. Just what I need to get all rested up for next semester."

"So why can't you just be yourself *and* nice?" I asked. "What's stopping you?"

"Because that's not me," he complained, the former distress returning to his face. "Everyone expects me to be all sweet and nice like their adorable big brother, but that's not *me*! I can't be you, Spencer, any more than you could enjoy making your family feel stupid all the time the way I'm so gifted."

"Well if you can't be nice, can't you just stop being sarcastic for a while?"

Ski's look of bewilderment returned and he shrugged his shoulders helplessly.

"Ya know what?" I asked, then paused to think. "I think I've finally figured you out. You've got everything you need, you're smart, you're about to graduate, everything's going your way, but you're always so sarcastic and negative. I think I figured out why."

Ski looked at me, an amused expression stretching across his face, one eyebrow raising, ready to laugh at whatever explanation I had come up with. "Oh, yeah? Why?"

"Everything's a game and it's always you against everyone else. But that's just a front. Something else is going on inside you." Ski raised another doubtful eyebrow at that. "You're hiding something," I accused.

"And exactly what am I hiding?" Ski asked, still smirking.

"That you're afraid, that's what," I answered, feeling more sure of myself with every word.

"Afraid?!" Ski asked, "Me? Of what?" An incredulous scoff replaced his smirk.

"I don't know," I answered. "Of something. So you always control the game by only playing by your rules," I accused, poking one finger into his chest to drive the point home. He swatted my hand away and shoved me backward, making me sit down on my bed.

"Oh, yeah?" Ski asked, still doubtful but no longer arguing. "What are my rules?"

"Sarcasm, mostly," I explained. "Nothing's ever serious. And you argue away any idea that doesn't fit into your picture of the world."

"If I win every argument, then maybe I *am* right. Ever consider that, Einstein?"

"Yeah, what-ever. If you're always right, then why can't you win by anyone else's rules?"

"What rules are those?" Ski probed. He suddenly looked a bit worried. It wasn't often that anyone found any chink in his armor.

"Other people's rules include things like sincerity. Genuineness. Caring and feeling. Connecting with people on more than just a…a…."

"A rhetorical level," Ski finished for me.

"Yeah. Exactly. More than just on a mental level, like life is nothing more than a philosophical story problem for you to solve."

Ski sat down on his own bed and pondered that for a moment. "Hmm," he said, more to himself than to me.

"Why would you do all this?" I asked, perplexed.

"You seem to be the one with all the answers today," Ski pointed out. "Why don't you tell me?"

I thought for a moment, watching as his expression shifted back and forth between curiosity and introspection to agitation and distress. "It's got to be some kind of defense system," I thought out loud. "So there must be something you don't want anyone to see or something you don't want to feel."

"Ha!" Ski laughed bitterly. "Are you saying that *I* have feelings?"

I looked at my friend and raised one eyebrow questioningly. "Are you saying you don't?"

"Are you saying," he said, suddenly thoughtful, "that I'm afraid of my own feelings?"

"It's true, isn't it?" I asked. "You're hiding something."

Ski stared at me as he considered the idea.

"It makes perfect sense, of course," I explained, "considering

The Perfect Gift

your family life. You were always handed off to nannies and boarding schools and never learned what it's like to be loved unconditionally. So rather than learn something new, you just keep gathering evidence to prove that you're right, that there's no such thing as love, and that the world is flat."

"Good one," Ski conceded. "Life would be pretty flat without love. And if you're right about all this..." Ski began, then paused again. I waited. "I've wasted a lot of time." Ski looked up at me then, questioning, it seemed, whether I was a true friend, whether I was right, and whether somebody could really be completely, permanently, unconditionally on his side.

He must have known the truth, but it must have been too much to consider all at once, because he just laughed once more, stood up, and strode out of the room. Downstairs, I heard the back door slam behind him.

14 Tin Man

I took a hot shower and walked outside. Ski sat on the edge of the porch, shivering. The sun had dropped toward the horizon and temperatures fell along with it.

"I can't take two weeks of this," he said. "Maybe I should catch a bus back home."

I sat down next to him and handed him the coat I was about to put on. I still felt warm from my shower and didn't need it. "That's the stupidest idea you've ever had," I told him.

We sat in silence for a moment, then Ski asked, "Well, aren't you going to tell me why?"

"You know why," I answered. "This is the best chance you'll ever have to alter your perspective. You could have a paradigm shift that would change your life, right here, in two short weeks. There's nowhere else in the world you could get as much attention and affection as right inside this house. Besides, what do you have to lose?"

"That's all true," he admitted, "but I just can't take it right now. I need a break first, I need some time to get used to the idea, to figure out how to deal with this."

"Tomorrow will be different," I said. "You'll see."

"I'm serious, Spence. I don't want to blow this right off the bat. Then I'll have to play catch up, too. I just need a little time away to get ready."

"Then come with me," I told him, standing up and walking toward the barn. "We'll chop some wood." Not only did physical activity always help me think—or at least clear my mind so the answers could come on their own—but I was growing cold without my coat. Chopping firewood would kill two birds with one stone.

Inside the barn, all the wood had already been chopped. I stared at the pile for a second, wondering what else we could do, and noticed that the wood pile was less than half full. I picked up the chainsaw and a gas can from a shelf and set them in the back of the truck. "We're going camping," I said, then walked back toward the house.

"What?"

"We'll cut down more wood and come back tomorrow."

Ski followed me into the house obediently as I gathered a tent, a pair of sleeping bags, some food, and my swimming suit. "Get yours," I told him.

"No way!" Ski objected. "I'm not doing one of those polar bear things through the ice!"

"Don't worry," I said. "Just get it."

"Ski and I are going up for more firewood!" I shouted into the living room as we walked out the back door.

"Right now?" someone asked. Night wasn't the normal time to go for wood, especially not in winter.

"I'd hate for us to run out on Christmas morning!" I answered. "See y'all tomorrow."

Before long the two of us sat in the truck, coasting along a gravel road toward the low foothills where wood cutting was allowed. The snow beneath the tires made the ride smooth and quiet.

Ski reached up and turned on the radio. When he discovered only AM stations playing country music or talking, he switched it back off and watched the road. "Thanks, Spence," he said. "I know you didn't really want to spend time away from your fam. You're a real pal."

"There'll be plenty of time to spend with everybody later on," I replied. Besides, I knew where we were going and it would be worth it.

Soon the ground turned dark to one side of the road. No snow clung to the ground here, and I steered the truck off the road and parked, then hopped out of the cab. "C'mon," I told Ski.

The ground was frozen underfoot and we followed the swath

The Perfect Gift

where no snow remained. Soon the ground grew soft and a cloud of vapor appeared before us. I pulled off my shoes and socks and carried them as the frozen earth turned to warm mud.

In the dark, I found a series of boards that acted as a makeshift walkway over the mud. The boards led to a rocky cliff with a ledge where I set my shoes and changed into my swimsuit. I was shivering violently but didn't mind since the cold wouldn't last long.

With Ski following behind, I walked along the ledge until we reached a pool of steaming water, completely hidden by its own vapor. I jumped in, my feet just touching the gravel and mud bottom.

Ahh, it felt wonderful! The not-quite-hot water smoothed away every goose bump on my body, and I swam the length of the pool—about thirty feet—then found a submerged ledge where I sat comfortably with most of my body below the warm surface.

Ski swam a dozen laps through the hot water before finding his own spot against the cliff. We both sat in silence, watching the steam rise and drift away into the night sky, toward the moon just rising over the horizon. I occasionally blew through the steam as if it were candles on a birthday cake, watching the mist swirl away from my pursed lips.

I had never camped at the hot springs in winter before, and now I wondered why not. *I should have come last year,* I thought to myself. *This would have been a nice spot to ring in the new year when the town dance got boring.*

With that thought, memories from last year came flooding back to mind. I floated in the warm water and let the thoughts float through my mind, remembering being at the dance, driving to Evanston with Annetta for midnight fireworks, tossing coins into the river, going cross-country skiing, and staying out all night next to a fire in the snow.

As I remembered Netta, I realized that I had hardly let myself think of her since I gave up hoping to hear from her last summer. Each time I thought of her or saw a face in a crowd that reminded me of her, I simply pushed the thought away.

That could explain my strange feelings in the forest this afternoon, I thought. All those buried feelings coming out at once, together with the creepy feelings I experienced, made me think of zombies rising from the dead. It would probably be wise to let them out now, so I could finish letting them go and they could die with the rising sun.

I let memories of last Christmas flow through my mind. I remembered meeting Netta when I stopped at the diner for a lemonade. I thought of my first date with her and the way she made me feel when I looked into her eyes. I didn't remember exactly what those feelings were, just that she was unique and made everything around us seem more interesting and alive.

I remembered how ridiculously happy she had made me feel for a few wonderfully happy days.

Sappy days, I reminded myself. It was just a crush that turned out to be nothing. Nothing at all. Nothing but disappointment and confusion.

I remembered days spent reading together in the library, nights sipping hot chocolate in the dark the café after closing time, and interesting conversations that went on forever and never tied up all the loose ends.

I remembered the night when her sister Amy and I waited out a blizzard inside a tiny snow cave, and Annetta sitting on the edge of my bed when I woke up the next morning, and how she finally opened her heart and allowed herself to fall for me then, and thAt first, of many kisses.

Surprisingly, the memory of kissing Netta began to melt a piece of my heart that had frozen last summer. It made the old pain and confusion and anger begin to evaporate and disappear, as if they never happened. It seemed to make everything okay between us again, and it seemed like letting go of those dark feelings was a very good idea. I would be happier and better able to get on with my life if I stopped avoiding them while actually carrying them around deep inside.

But it didn't seem right to be dreaming about kissing Netta when I had Julie, so I shifted my thoughts to something else.

I thought over the things Netta had taught me. That courage and love form the secret to a meaningful and purposeful life. Love conquers fear, and courage gets you through while waiting for the fear to vanish.

Now I wished we could discuss it all over again. I wished we could just talk and let everything go so I could start completely fresh with no questions from the past to haunt me. I wished Netta could be here to spend a night in the hot springs…*Wait*, I quickly corrected myself, *I wish* Julie *could be here*.

But she wasn't. I'd have to settle for talking with Ski.

"So, Ski," I asked, growing tired of my own thoughts at last, "what would you say is the meaning of life these days?"

The Perfect Gift

"Life? Enjoy it," he said absent-mindedly.

If every day in life could be spent sitting in a hot spring, and if you would never grow tired of it, that might work. Except that every hot spring in the world would get terribly over crowded. So can you simply enjoy every moment, no matter where you are? No matter what you're doing? Can you simply *decide* to be happy? I wondered if the solution could be so simple.

"So can you just *decide* to be happy?" I asked. "How do you do it?"

"Not happy," Ski answered. "That's different."

"What's the difference?"

"The difference is that happiness is a myth. People talk about it as something you can get a grip on and never let go, but you can't. Anyone who tries figures that out eventually. Happiness is a result of doing certain things. Any old philosopher will tell you that— Plato, Aristotle, John Stuart Mills, everybody."

Ski pushed away from the wall and coasted across the pond again. He disappeared into the vapor, but his voice still sounded close. "Anyway, focusing on the feeling and clinging too tightly makes you forget what you did to get the feeling in the first place. Then it slips away."

"So what's the difference?" I asked again. "What's different about enjoying life?"

"Being happy is trying to *be* something. Enjoying is *doing* something. If you're having a bad day, you can't necessarily turn happy just because you want to, but you can always go do something enjoyable."

"And that's as good as being happy?" I asked. It still didn't sound right.

"No," Ski answered. "I didn't say that."

"Is it better than being happy?"

"No. Being happy is better."

"Then why do you say that enjoying life is the meaning of life, and not happiness?"

"Well I was giving you *my* meaning of life."

"Oh, so the meaning of life changes for each person?" I asked.

"Listen, Spence, if you want happiness to be your meaning of life, then that's great. Go for it. But for me, it just doesn't work. For birds, the meaning of life might be to fly around. But if you're a fish, you might as well forget it. See what I mean?"

I remembered our discussion back at school. "So it's

impossible for you to be happy?" I asked.

"Yep."

"Why?" I still didn't believe it. I thought he was just being stubborn.

"Because I'm the tin man, that's why."

"The tin man?" I asked. "You don't have a heart?"

"Yeah, that's right. And there's no Wizard of Oz handing them out."

"The wizard never gave the tin man a heart. Just a stupid piece of paper."

"You think I don't know that? You think I'm an idiot? Of course I already have a heart, but I can't use it, not like that. I've read a dozen of those stupid, cheesy self-improvement books this semester trying to figure it out, but their ideas don't work, not on me. My head works fine, my brain's not the problem. That's why we're here, remember? So I can decide if this vacation has any chance of teaching me something or if I should just have you drop me off at the Greyhound station tomorrow morning."

"You've been reading self-help books?" I asked, surprised. When Ski didn't answer, I asked, "Why?"

"Because if I don't figure this out," Ski explained impatiently, "I'm going to end up unhappy and alone forever."

That made sense. Ski was lucky to have a few friends who happily tolerated him, but he never let anyone else get close. Eventually Julie and I would get busy with our lives and family and we wouldn't have as much time to spend with him. If he didn't learn to open his heart, there was no guarantee he would ever replace us. I could hardly imagine how lonely life would become without true friends.

Despite Ski's claim that he had no heart, I didn't believe him. I knew him well enough to know he had a heart and I was determined to prove him wrong.

"Think back to this morning," I said. "Remember the first thing you said to me?"

"That your Grandma's place was beautiful," Ski answered. "So what?"

"Well, you can't appreciate beauty without your heart," I answered, "so you see, your heart isn't totally useless."

"Not true," Ski countered. I heard him take a deep breath, then sink under water. All was silent for a moment until he surfaced at the far end and came swimming back toward the cliff edge. "That's my brain. I don't know how I know that, since I don't know what it's like to feel with my heart, but I know it's different. I guess I'm just smart enough to at least recognize that the view out of the window belonged on a calendar."

"Well what about those people we talked to in Salt Lake? I don't care what you say, you really cared about them and were trying to make them feel better. You can't tell me you can care about people without a heart."

"Oh, sure, a little; that's easy. I'm not a *monster*, you know. It's the bigger things. Like spending two weeks with a bunch of people I don't even know who expect me to be all nice and friendly and like family. I can't connect with that. I don't know how. That's the sort of thing I'm talking about. It's too much." He pushed off from the cliff again and drifted away.

As always, once Ski explained his point of view, I found it making a lot of sense. Still, I wasn't ready to give up just yet. "So what about me? Do you connect with me?"

Ski floated silently somewhere out in the vapor. I heard him take another deep breath and plunge beneath the surface again. He stayed under for longer this time, over a minute, finally surfacing near the spot he first went under, breathing hard. He must have swam the length of the pool and back. He waited to catch his breath again before speaking. "Yeah, I guess I do."

"So what's the difference?" I asked.

"I was just wondering the same thing," Ski answered. "You *know* me, for one thing."

"Yeah, but didn't we connect pretty well even before I knew you that well?" We met in class a year and a half ago and had gotten along great from the start.

"Yeah, I guess so."

"So what's the difference?"

"Shut up," Ski said. "I'm thinking."

I pushed away from the wall and coasted across the surface, then dove and swam until I reached the far side and my fingers plunged into the muddy bottom. I stood up and let the warm, dark muck ooze between my toes. The water only reached to my knees here and the cold air felt refreshing, momentarily. I stood in the air until goose bumps rose across my shoulders and chest and I began to shiver, then dove back in, the warm water against my skin erasing all discomfort.

I swam back to the cliff beyond where the ledge ended and began to climb the cold, damp rock, knowing the water would catch me safely if I slipped, would warm me if I grew too cold.

"Hey," I yelled, "I know what it is! The difference is trust! Isn't it?"

"Are you saying I don't trust your family?" Ski asked.

"I'm saying you don't trust *anybody*."

"Why wouldn't I trust anyone? It's not like they can do anything to hurt me."

"Of course not, not as long as you stay disconnected from them. That way no one comes into contact with whatever's really important to you—and whatever's vulnerable."

"Vulnerable? Like what?"

"How would I know?" I asked. "I don't think I've ever seen it!"

"I don't know, Spence. This isn't making much sense."

"All right, then," I said, "let's do a little test."

"Fire away."

"Tell me something that makes you uncomfortable."

"Nothing makes me uncomfortable," Ski answered. "What were you expecting?"

"There are a few things you never talk about. Like religion. Why don't you ever want to talk about that?"

"It's not because it makes me uncomfortable. I just don't have anything to say about it."

"See what I mean? You have something to say about everything else."

"You're striking out here, Spencer. Maybe I just don't know enough about it to have a solid opinion, so I keep my mouth shut."

"Yeah, okay, maybe you're right. What about your parents, how come you never talk about your family?"

"You know they're not exactly a big part of my life. And vice versa. So what would I have to say about that? That's two strikes, Spence. One more and the test ends."

"Doesn't it bother you that your parents have never been that close to you?"

"Why should I care? I can take care of myself just fine."

"But don't you think that has something to do with why you don't really connect with anyone else?"

"Sure, maybe. Why not? But it doesn't make me uncomfortable to talk about. It doesn't make me feel vulnerable. Why are we taking this test, anyway?"

"To show you what trust means and see if you can do it or not."

"Well, you've got one more chance."

The Perfect Gift

"Okay, give me a second. There's got to be something." I climbed up on the ledge and stood dripping in the cool air again. The cold sharpened my mind a bit, but still nothing came to me. "All right then, you tell me. What's the one secret you have never told me?"

Ski pushed off backward from where he had been standing near the ledge and floated away into the fog. "Good question, Spencer; finally."

When the goose bumps spreading across my chest and arms caught my attention again, I realized that I had been standing with my mouth open, shocked at the revelation that Ski had kept some secret from me. I wondered what it might be.

Ski laughed through the vapor. "Catch 22. Now I either tell you my little secret or you win and prove that I don't really trust you."

I jumped into the water, doing my best cannonball. The water always felt best after standing in the cold. I surfaced and wiped the mineral water from my face. I still couldn't see Ski. "So which is it gonna be?" I asked.

"I think I'm going to tell you," he answered. I heard him duck underwater again, then surface near the ledge. He leaned against the cliff and stretched his arms along the ledge behind him. "You ready for this?" he asked.

"Fire away," I answered, curious.

"I want your girl."

Although I had absolutely no idea what to expect him to say, this was definitely not it. "You want *Julie*?" I asked.

"That's what I said."

"Why?"

"Oh, don't be stupid!" Ski almost shouted. "Who wouldn't want her? She's perfect!"

Things began falling into place in my mind. I remembered how her presence so often cheered him up, and how he sometimes grew silent when Julie would pour out any affection on me. How happy he was the morning we left school after spending a couple hours with her alone, along with the hug and a kiss on the cheek. And the way he never wanted to spend much time as a trio. "Well, I can see why you wouldn't want to tell me that," I admitted.

"Oh, there's no need to worry about it, though," he assured me. "It could never work out with us."

"Why not?" I asked.

"You know—the tin man thing."

Shaun Roundy

"Oh," I said, "I thought for a minute that you loved her."

"I do. I wouldn't want her if I didn't!"

I paused. "And how does that make you feel?" I swam through the steam to where I thought Ski was and wondered if he had dived below the surface again. Then suddenly he stood right in front of me, barely visible in the dim starlight.

"Hmm," he said, pursing his lips. "That's my heart?"

I didn't know whether to be happy or sad. Here my best friend was experiencing one of the most significant breakthroughs of his life, but it involved him having feelings for *my* girlfriend who would soon become my fiancée and then my wife.

But what did I have to worry about? *I* was the one she loved. *I* was the one in love with her. I was the one with the diamond ring all ready to slip onto her finger and claim her forever. And hadn't Ski even been instrumental in getting us together? I had nothing to fear, least of all from Ski.

15 Trust & Hearts

"What do I do now?" Ski asked.

"Learn to feel, it sounds like."

"So," Ski said, "when do my lessons start?"

"Whenever you're ready," I answered.

"All right, teacher, I'm ready. Let's begin."

"Oh, I'm no teacher," I objected. "You'll have to figure this out by yourself."

"Yeah, right. As if I have any idea how to do that."

"Well," I thought, "I guess whenever you feel your heart, hang on to that feeling. Get to know it. Let it grow."

"And I'll know that when it comes?"

"I think so. It's like the way you feel about Julie, right?"

"And you expect me to feel that way about everyone? That's highly unlikely."

"Well it doesn't have to be exactly like that," I said. "It's like these hot springs. It's just a little heat escaping from under the earth's crust. When you feel something like this bubbling up, you'll know, and it'll feel even better than paddling around in this mud hole. Does that make sense?"

"Not really. And I don't know why it should suddenly start working after all this time, or if I'd recognize it if it did."

The Perfect Gift

"Come here," I said, getting an idea.

"What for?" Ski asked.

"Just come here," I answered. "You'll see."

Ski swam toward me, then stopped and waited. Before he could react, I reached out and punched him hard in the chest, just under the water, sending warm water splashing into his face.

"What was that for?! And you're trying to teach me *trust*?!" Ski lifted his right arm half way out of the water, deciding whether or not to hit me back.

"Can you feel that? Where I hit you?" I asked.

"Yeah. What's the point? 'Cause you'd better come up with one quick!"

"That's to remind you where to focus. Focus on that spot and try to feel or think and see what happens. Maybe that will help you to begin an awareness of how your heart feels." I didn't know if it would work or not. I hadn't really thought about it, just acted as soon as the idea came. Now it was beginning to seem kind of stupid and rash. I hoped Ski would lower his fist.

Ski leaned backward and floated slowly away from me. I let myself sink until my mouth and eyes hovered just above the water's surface.

"It hurts where you hit me," Ski said.

I stood back up and leaned against the cliff again. "Sorry about that, man," I answered. "I didn't mean to hit you so hard."

"No," Ski said, softer. "It hurts on the *inside*."

"Are you having a heart attack or something?"

"No, you stupid idiot!" he said, shouting again. "It's like, pain. It's like an ache. It's like it makes me want to cry or something."

I didn't know how to take this news, and had no idea how to react. So I didn't, I just sat in the steam and waited. Twenty minutes passed in silence as we each drifted along with our own thoughts. The only sounds were occasional splashes as we swam slowly or dived. I kept wondering if it was my turn to talk, but every time I opened my mouth to say something, that something seemed weak and pointless, so I let my mouth close again and waited.

The steam muffled all sound, somehow blocking out the rest of the world with its mist, making this the perfect place to think without interruption. Every once in a while, I heard Ski sniff through the steam.

"Ya know what?" Ski said, finally breaking the silence. "The pain feels kind of good."

Once again I didn't know how to respond. I didn't want to interrupt Ski's thoughts and growth or healing or whatever was going on inside him.

"How does it feel to be the Wizard?" he asked.

"The what?"

"The Wizard of Oz," he answered.

"You found your heart?"

"Yeah, I think I did. With a little help from my best friend."

Again, I was silent for a moment. "If you make it home, Toto, it won't be my fault."

"Speaking of home, are we going to stay here all night?"

"Maybe. Do you think you can sleep in here?"

We tried for a while, piling rocks in the mud at the edges of the pool and resting our heads there, letting our bodies float weightlessly. But the cold air that breathed against our chests wouldn't let us doze for long. Finally we climbed out and dried off as quickly as possible, dressed and ran to the truck, then set up the tent on the snow, which felt softer than the frozen mud.

By the time we curled up in our sleeping bags, I was tired and ready for sleep. I had no idea what time it was, but it had been a very long day.

"What's it like having a heart to use all the time?" Ski asked in the darkness.

"What do you mean?"

"I read this book a few months ago— The Art of Heart—about this girl who figures out you can know things with your heart just like you know with your brain. Only the things you know with your heart are supposedly even more sure, even if you don't understand them At first,." Ski paused, then looked at me. I more sensed than saw his eyes looking at me in the darkness. "Well?" he asked.

"Well what?"

"What's it like knowing things with your heart?"

"I don't know," I answered. "I mean, I know a few things that way, but they all have to do with my religion. Like when you pray, sometimes you just *know* God is listening. But I never thought of using that to know other things."

"And how do you know that stuff about God listening?" Ski inquired.

"You just feel it. It's like you get filled with this peace and joy and excitement, and…" I tried to remember the feeling, tried to put words to it. "And strength. And you just know it's not coming from yourself, so it must be from God."

"Hmm," Ski merely answered in the darkness.

"You don't believe me, do you?" I asked.

"I don't know what to think. I don't have any experience with it, so I don't have an opinion."

As Ski's breathing deepened and became a light snore, sleep evaded me. I started wondering about knowing other things with my heart. Was it possible? What kinds of things could I know? How would I recognize if my heart was trying to tell me something? Inside my own sleeping bag I reached up and touched my chest, then pictured Julie's face, wondering if my heart had any messages to tell me about her.

The only thought that came to me was that I missed her. I wished she could be near to talk to and hold. I missed her bright eyes and quick mind, and no matter how much I was enjoying the holidays, I would be glad when they ended, or at least when Julie came back.

What would happen then, I wondered. I touched my chest again and tried to listen to my heart, but before I found any answers, I drifted off to dreamland and the question floated away into the dark night sky, rising with the steam from the nearby pool.

16 Stuck

The hard, frozen snow below the tent trembled early the next morning when a truck rattled up the road past our camp. The sky had grown light by then, but we waited to get up until the sun warmed the tent enough to make it, not comfortable, but bearable to climb out of our sleeping bags.

We packed up the tent, took the chainsaw and ax from the truck bed, and walked up the road toward a stand of dead trees. I pulled the chainsaw cord a few times and sawdust flew everywhere as the chain dug into dry tree trunks. Ski cleared off dead branches with the ax, then stacked the wood into piles.

By the time we had cut a truck-full of wood, the day had grown warm enough that we could take off our coats as long as we kept working. The fresh air cooled our sweat while the sun warmed our bare skin.

"That should do," I said. "Let's haul it down to the truck and get home for some breakfast."

"I have a better idea," Ski responded, "why don't we just

drive the truck over here?"

I nodded and set the saw down on the snow. The ground back at the truck had thawed and I took my time jumping from one rock to another, managing to make my way to the cab without covering my shoes with too much mud.

The engine started and I put it in reverse and let the clutch out slowly. Without moving an inch, I felt the rear wheels break free and spin. I pushed in the clutch and tried again, this time giving it less gas. For a moment I thought I'd make it out, but then the wheels spun again. I opened the door and looked back to find the rear wheels sitting two inches deeper than before in the black mud.

I shifted into first to rock the truck back and forth and build some momentum, but again, the truck would not budge. I shifted into neutral and hopped out to lock the front wheel hubs into four-wheel drive, giving up on keeping my shoes clean. Dark mud had already splattered all over the sides of the white truck, kicked up by the spinning tires.

I was surprised when my feet instantly sank three inches into the mud. Rising temperatures had allowed the warm water from the springs to turn our parking place into a bog. "Great," I muttered to myself, but didn't begin to worry. One way or another, we'd make it out of here.

I walked around the truck and locked the hubs, then climbed back in and shifted into four-wheel drive. Even in low, the truck only barely inched forward as the tires spun up mud. I moved backward three inches to get a rocking motion started, but quickly realized that this only allowed the truck to sink still deeper. Finally I shut off the engine and climbed out.

"Hey, Ski! Bring a few of the big branches down here, we're stuck!"

Ski complied, but let me do all the walking through the mud to place the branches beneath the tires for extra traction. When I climbed in the truck and tried again, I thought for a moment that it would work. But as soon as the sticks were pressed into the mud, their smooth surfaces became slippery and the tires spun again, throwing still more mud into the air.

"I don't remember the truck being two-tone," Ski commented. The dark brown mud complimented the white paint rather nicely.

After twenty minutes trying to ease the truck atop these branches, I had only succeeded in creating four holes to collect pools of water around the wheels. I could hardly jam the sticks low enough to work them in beneath the tires.

I shut off the engine and shrugged my shoulders toward Ski, who shouted back "There is no *try*, young Skywalker! There is only *do!*" I laughed and climbed out of the stranded x-wing, sloshing carelessly through the mud to the edge of the snow where Ski stood watching. I sat down on a rock and closed my eyes, hoping a new idea would occur to me.

"I feel like I've lost something" Ski said.

"If it's anywhere in that mud," I answered, "you'll never see it again." When Ski didn't say anything, I asked, "What did you lose?"

"Ya know all that stuff we talked about last night?" he began.

"Yeah?"

"I actually believed it would work for a while. I've never felt so good. Thanks for that."

"Are you saying you don't believe it anymore?"

"Yeah. I've been trying to get it back all morning, but it's gone. I remember everything but it just doesn't come. So it must have just been excitement about the possibilities."

"Want me to hit you again?" I asked helpfully.

"Go ahead," Ski whispered back in his best Clint Eastwood impression. "Make my day."

I thought for a minute longer. "This isn't something that happens all at once, ya know. It's like spring. Today's a warm day, right? So now you suddenly expect to have leaves growing on the trees already, birds singing all around, and rabbits humming 'Zippideedoodah?' It just doesn't happen that fast."

I kept my eyes closed and let the warm sun pour down on my face.

"Thanks, Spencer," Ski finally said. "That did the trick. I think if I can make myself believe in it, then the feeling comes back. I don't know if it'll really work, but even if it never does, I'm happy with just hoping it will work and feeling this way for a while."

"I wouldn't worry about it. If you feel that way now, then it's working. You'll be just fine after a few more warm days."

"Yeah, warm days have done us a lot of good today. We're hopelessly stuck with no way to escape unless we wait for the mud to freeze up again tonight. I'm beginning to feel like I'll starve to death before that happens."

"I guess it's time to get started on Plan B," I said.

"Which is?"

"You may have to change some of the ways you get around."

"Are you talking about me or the truck?"

"Either one, I guess."

"Let's discuss one at a time. What about me? Are you saying I need to change something? Are you saying I am anything less than absolutely, utterly, one-hundred-percent perfect?"

"I didn't have anything in mind, but now that you mention it, a drop of humility might be a nice addition."

"You are *so* right!" Ski mocked. "I have been nothing but proud and arrogant! Can you ever, *ever* forgive me?"

"And then there's your sarcasm. That definitely has to go."

Ski opened his mouth, ready with his next comeback, but hesitated, then closed his mouth altogether. "Really?"

"Do whatever you want, Ski; but if you really want to feel everything fully then you'll need to have enough courage to be genuine."

Ski thought about that for a moment. "But only sometimes, right?"

"Sure. How would I know? I guess as long as you know you *can* do it, as long as it's always an option, then you're doing okay."

Ski thought for a moment longer, then asked, "Has my sarcasm ever bothered you?"

"No," I answered, laying back on the snow. "I think I've always had a pretty good idea of what you really mean and feel. But other people might not. And if you want really good relationships, you're going to have to be willing to let down that guard and be vulnerable sometimes, don't you think?"

"Didn't we already decide last night that nothing really bothers me? That I'm not vulnerable?"

"You're right. That's great. Then you shouldn't have any trouble being genuine and open, should you?"

We sat in the snow for a while longer in silence. Soon a cloud covered the sun and I felt the chill of the air. "We should probably get started on plan B," I said.

"You never finished explaining," Ski answered.

"Plan B means walking home. Or at least far enough to get some help."

"How far is that?"

"Not too far," I answered. "Shouldn't take more than an hour or two."

"You call that not far?" Ski asked, then added, "Ya know, I'm getting a lot out of just sitting here. Mind going alone? Someone should stay and guard the wood pile, ya know."

"I have an idea," I said, "why don't you guard the woodpile and I'll walk to town?"

"Go on without me," Ski answered dramatically. "Leave me! Save yourself! But could you grab me some food from the truck before you leave?"

"Why don't you just make yourself a bridge with sticks through the mud? It'll give you something to do."

"Good idea. I bet you wish you'd have thought of that."

I looked down at my mud-caked shoes and nodded my head, then stood up. "See ya in a couple hours," I said, stepping onto the frozen road and stomping my feet in a futile attempt to shake off the mud.

17 Hibernation

The sun shone brightly on the snowy hills beautifully enough that I felt content, At first,, to walk along the road and not think about anything. My boots made a musical squeaky crunching with each step as hundreds of tiny snow crystals snapped, collapsing under my weight.

Along the roadside, leafless aspens cut sharp, jagged lines across the blue sky dotted with fluffy white clouds.

The trees looked dead, but of course they were only sleeping, hibernating, drawing within themselves and waiting out the frozen winter. If they didn't shed their leaves, ice and snow would build up and the weight would snap their thin branches.

When the days grew longer again and the snow melted away, their time would come to thrive again. The trees would regenerate, sprouting new leaves to quiver in springtime breezes.

The birds would return as well, their tireless little wings carrying them back from warm Central American beaches, and their music would chase away winter's silence.

I glanced down from the rolling foothills and saw the distant town at the far end of the Amber Valley. The highway cut a thin, dark line across the snow. I saw Becca's Diner, the high school, cemetery, church, library, and the street where Netta and her family had lived.

I thought of how she had flown away to Marseilles, on the French Riviera. Unlike the robins and sparrows, though, she would not return in the spring.

I thought also about how she had flown out of my life without a word at the first hint of chill in the air and cold days to come. Perhaps she knew that her tender branches wouldn't survive a winter storm and drew inside to avoid breaking. Maybe she knew that even before we got involved and that's why she resisted me for so long.

I knew she was wrong to do so – humans aren't meant to hibernate. When it grows cold outside, we shouldn't fall asleep until winter has passed. Instead, we should huddle together and keep each other warm.

But if she was that vulnerable and delicate, if she did what she had to do to survive, then I guess I couldn't blame her.

In the end, she had been an exciting but brief crush that brought me more sorrow than joy, and yet...yet...I couldn't bring myself to wish her away, to wish she never happened to me.

The few days we had together were so sweet. She was so unique. In those few days, she left her impression on me and changed me forever. Even if she turned out to be a flake, I had to admit that I loved her.

And what surprised me to notice was that...I *still* loved her. How could I help it? She really was a wonderful girl, and she had a good effect on me, and there was no use denying it.

I resisted these feelings, looking for the resentment to recreate the barrier between us so I could forget her again and move on in a different direction. But not only had I allowed myself to remember her too clearly since returning to Amber, I had reached a new understanding that let me forgive her, and the barrier would not return to shield me from loving her.

And maybe that was okay. Despite all the bad memories, maybe the whole experience had been worth going through. Maybe the bad outnumbers the good, but the good outweighs the bad.

I sighed as I walked along the road. I didn't want to deal with such complex thinking. I wanted *one* thing, I wanted Julie, and I wanted everything to remain clear. Then again, it didn't really matter. I could love more than one person. It didn't mean I had to do anything about it, it didn't mean I loved Julie any less. Letting myself love Netta didn't hurt anything besides making me think too much, so I guess that would be okay, too.

18 Starting Over

I walked for another half hour and let my thoughts wander aimlessly. I stared across the valley, and various buildings, roads and fields sparked memories from recent and long-ago days.

I allowed myself to continue thinking about Netta more than I had for months. I remembered our first date, the school play. I remembered wandering the halls and talking during intermission. I remembered crossing the bridge on the way back to the car and tossing coins into the river. I remembered the way she squeezed my hand as I dropped her off and how I thought my wishes were coming true.

I remembered two weeks later as we said goodbye. We sat at a booth in the dark café and held each other, confessing our affection and hopes for the future. I remembered how her arms felt around my neck and her lips against my ear.

No, that was too much. I should be thinking of kissing Julie and no one else. I thought back to our goodbye two days ago, the way Julie tugged my textbook from my lap and took its place. I remembered the way she draped herself around my shoulders and kissed me softly.

Then once again, Netta's face appeared in my mind, only this time she was not kissing me.

"Go right ahead," she dared me. "Make your wish." She looked angry. And hurt. And accusing. "Wish for anything. What do you really want?" she taunted.

I recognized my guilty conscious talking. She didn't want to get involved in the first place, but I talked her into it. She didn't want to set herself up for certain disappointment and heartbreak later, but I convinced her that it would be worth it.

Then the minute I got back to school, Julie had been there, waiting to snatch me up. I resisted until Netta quit writing, but in the end, maybe Netta was right. Maybe her worst fears had come true after all.

That could explain why she didn't write. Maybe she knew her leaves and branches couldn't support the weight of heavy snow, so she drew herself in, saving her strength for warmer days to come.

Maybe she even blamed me. Maybe she read between the lines what I wouldn't yet admit even to myself, that Julie and I were getting too close, that we would eventually fall in love, and that Netta would lose me forever.

But that's life - all's fair in love and war. You win some and you lose even more.

But despite such rationalizations, if Netta really withdrew to avoid the hurt from losing me…then I couldn't help but feel a little sorry for her.

And maybe…maybe in a way she was right. Maybe I had let her down. I encouraged her to make wishes for herself, to hope, and then, no matter whose fault it was, her dreams didn't come true.

I'm sorry, I told Netta in my mind. *Things don't always work out the way you plan. That's not my fault. But I'm sorry if I hurt you.*

Her face vanished again from my mind and left me walking down the snow-covered road alone.

It surprised me to notice that I felt even better than before. Happier. Lighter.

Then I understood. All along, I had blamed Annetta for our drifting apart. That blame made me feel bitter. All my resistance, my insistence that I had totally given up on her, only proved that I was not completely over her. That we had unfinished business, at least within my heart.

I had learned to forgive her, but complete healing required more. Admitting my fault in the matter, no matter how small or innocent, and asking forgiveness for that completed the circle.

Now I felt complete. Now I could let go of the past and leave it completely behind me. Now I could start over with a clean slate, and again I felt surprised to notice how happy that made me feel.

19 Homecoming

I had walked about a mile when I heard a truck engine behind me. Ski must have taken the time to load more wood and rocks beneath the tires and made it out after all. I should have tried harder before giving up. I turned around and was surprised to see an orange truck appear from behind the rise in the road.

I recognized the truck immediately and held out one thumb to hitch a ride. The truck slowed to a stop next to me as the driver's window rolled down, spilling a crackly country song from his radio onto the snow-packed road. "Howdy, stranger," the driver said.

"How are you, Jim?"

Jim reached out a hand wearing a well-worn leather work glove and I shook it.

Grandpa's muddy white truck came roaring over the hill

The Perfect Gift

behind us just then with Ski at the wheel. He stomped on the gas momentarily, then locked up its brakes and slid to a stop behind Jim.

"Thanks for pulling that out," I said, nodding toward the truck.

"What comes around goes around," he answered. I nodded knowingly at his reference to last winter. I had found Annetta's sister Amy stuck, freezing on a snowmobile in a blizzard, then crashed mine into a drift to create a snow cave to keep her warm and later get her home safely. "You sure got a knack for choosing parking spots," he smiled.

"Live and learn, I guess."

"How've ya been?" he asked sincerely. Something about his tone or manner made it clear that this wasn't just a hollow question. He really wanted to know. He didn't expect me to answer 'fine' if it wasn't the absolute truth, and his authentic country charm struck me as odd or old fashioned in such a cynical world, but refreshingly so.

"Really good," I answered.

Jim nodded and thought about that for a moment. "Sure is great being in love, isn't it?" he asked. Ski must have told him all about Julie. "You must be excited," he added.

"Yeah, I am," I answered. I watched his face to see if there would be any trace of jealousy or resentment, any trace of irony that I more or less dashed his hopes for anything to happen between him and Netta last year and now I had moved on to someone else. But all I saw on Jim's honest face was sincerity and good will.

"Won't be long now till she's back," Jim said with a happy smile.

"Yeah," I agreed. The week would fly by. "But it still seems like a long time."

"I know just what you mean," he agreed. Now he looked forward through the windshield, focusing on nothing in particular, nodding his head slowly. "Keep busy and the time'll pass before ya know it," he advised.

This all sounded a bit serious for such a short wait. I chalked it up to Jim's friendly nature and had nothing left to say.

"Yer feet must be growin' cold just standin' there," Jim finally said. "Let's get goin'."

"Yeah, let's," I said. I slapped the door panel once and walked back toward Ski, climbing into the passenger side.

"That's Jim," I said.

"I know," Ski told me. "Friendly guy," he noted after I slammed the door shut.

"Sure is," I nodded. I remembered him from last year as a gentleman, but I hadn't seen him looking quite this happy.

"I'm not sure I've ever met anyone quite that friendly," he continued.

"Uh huh," I agreed.

"So the whole time he was helping pull the truck out and load the wood into the back, I was trying to figure out what makes him so happy."

"Did you find out anything?" I asked.

"No. He just kept smiling and working and commenting on how 'you certainly chose a fine day to get stuck in the mud' and such."

We followed Jim's truck the whole way back to Grandma's. If he was just making sure we got there safely, he was going a little far.

We parked the truck near the barn as Jim climbed out of his truck just in front of us. Before he had even slammed the door shut, my twenty-one-year-old cousin Kellie burst out of the house and came running straight for him. Jim caught her in his arms and swung her around once, laughing. When they stopped spinning, Kellie planted a great big, long, wet kiss right on Jim's mouth.

I had stopped with only one foot out of the truck and now turned toward Ski, also half way out his door.

"Well, that explains things," he muttered.

20 Feel

Jim stayed for dinner and I found out that he and Kellie had just gotten engaged. She had come up to stay with Grandma for the summer and things with Jim had fallen right into place. Jim would be moving to Alpine, near Jackson Hole, in a few months, where he had a job lined up at his friend's mechanic shop. He also had a connection with a Teton guide company where one good-tipping customer would pay as much as a month of small engine repair. Kellie would join him there once things got set up next summer.

"I guess this makes us cousins," I told Jim. "Welcome to the family!"

"It's great the way things tend ta work out on their own, ain't it? How are things goin' with you 'n Netta, anyways?" he asked as he heaped a second helping of candied yams onto his plate.

"They're not," I answered, surprised that he didn't know. I guess Ski hadn't filled him in after all.

Jim set the serving spoon back in the pan and looked up at me. "Didn't you just say…? I thought you said…."

"I was talking about Julie," I told him. "I have a pretty serious girlfriend back in school."

"Oh," Jim said, pursing his lips and cocking his head to one side. "I'm sorry to hear that." Then after another moment, "I mean, I'm happy to hear that. I'm glad things are going well for ya." He looked more perplexed than happy to hear the news. Dinner conversation continued around us as before but I noticed that Jim remained silent for the next few minutes.

After dinner, Ski slipped out to the back porch and I followed. The moon was just rising over the horizon, casting light shadows across the snow. "How you doing?" I asked. "You gonna be okay here now?"

"Yeah, sure," Ski answered. "No problem. Maybe I can learn a thing or two. Now I feel like I'm on some kind of sociology field trip or study abroad."

We stood there for a minute longer, looking out over the snowy fields, and I was just about to make my way back inside when Ski spoke again.

"I think I know what to do now." When I didn't say anything, he continued. "At least I know what to try. I don't know how well I'll do at it, but I sort of have a plan. I'm beginning to see possibilities I never considered before."

"Like what?" I asked, half out of curiosity and half because I could tell Ski wanted to talk it out, to say it out loud and make it more clear and real in his mind.

Ski thought for a moment and then spoke. "Possibilities about how life can be, I'd say. I always thought most happy people were shallow and foolish, so I never bothered to understand what it would be like to live in their heads. Ever since Jim showed up this afternoon, I've been watching him, and now I'm watching everyone else, too. And I'm seeing something I had missed."

He pursed his lips in thought, raised one eyebrow and then the other. "Happiness. Even shallow, foolish people can be happy — which is not to say that everyone here's shallow," he added, pausing to make sure I hadn't misunderstood. "Maybe being happy is better than being smart or right. But most importantly, I finally have a tiny shred of an idea of how it would feel to be happy, and if

I can feel that, then I know it can grow and I can figure it out. Does that make sense?"

"Sure," I assured him.

"I think the hardest part," Ski continued, "is the idea that there's more to me than just my body and brain. Who'd have thought?!" he sighed, then laughed out loud. "Thought—ha! That's exactly the problem, isn't it? It's not about thinking everything out, it's about learning to feel."

The laugh seemed to come from somewhere a little deeper down inside him than just his throat.

21 The Best Made Plans

When I checked my e-mail before bed, I had two messages waiting from Julie.

Dear Spence,

I miss you, too! I don't know what I was thinking – how could I ever have wanted to spend two whole weeks away from you?!

Missing you is...strange! It's more than I expected. On one hand, it's awful, but also so sweet! I can hardly wait to see you.

How's Ski doing with your family? I don't know why, but I imagine him struggling a little, for maybe for the first time in his life. In a way I want to laugh imagining him squirm, but I would never do that. Poor thing. I hope he survives!

I think he was really excited to go with you. He surprised me and took me out to breakfast before I left and he looked happier than I had seen him all semester! I was so glad to see him feeling better. He had seemed so down.

It's nice having the whole family together here, but so crowded! It's next to impossible to get any time by myself. Tomorrow I'm driving to the ocean - alone! I'm going to spend at least an hour walking along the dunes and watching the surf and thinking about you. It will be cold, but beautiful! I wish you could be there with me :(.

Janie (my seven-year-old sister) is whining that it's her turn on the computer, so I'll go for now.

I love you love you love you love you!!!
Julie

Her second message was shorter:

Tell me when you can pick me up in Salt Lake and I will be there!
I love you!!!

I read the messages over and over. I couldn't wait to bring Julie here, introduce her to the family, show her around the valley, and take her snowmobiling and skiing and to the hot pots.

I clicked "reply" and started typing.

Dear Julie,
You know I want you here tonight, and that I would pick you up any time, but I don't want to be selfish and steal you away from your family so soon. I mean, I DO want to be selfish, but I will restrain myself. So how about the 27th? Does that give you enough time there? Whatever works for you.

I can't wait to see you! You're going to love it here! I have so much to show you. You're going to love everyone and everyone is going to love you even more.

You were absolutely right about Ski! He was having a hard time At first,, but I think he's getting the hang of it. I think he's even learning a thing or two that he didn't expect. Ha! To think he expected to resist my family's influence! Impossible.

Okay. Tell me when you're coming and I'll pick you up. And tell me how your walk on the beach went. Sorry I couldn't join you (I really mean it).

I love you.
Spencer

22 Heart vs. Head

The next evening we attended the annual high school play. This year they did *Man of La Mancha*. Some of the actors were good, some of the songs beautiful, but just like last year, the most charming aspect came in the performers' enthusiasm and the appreciation returned from the small-town audience filling the auditorium.

When the play ended, we all made our way outside to the parking lot slowly, taking time to mingle and chit chat with neighbors. Many of the towns people remembered me from last year and came by to say hello, shake my hand, or slap me on the shoulder.

"Planning on doing any snowmobiling this year?" someone asked.

"Wouldn't miss it," I assured them.

"Then we'll see you there." They each gave me a knowing look and a nod as if to acknowledge that they remembered last year's incident with Amy and were still grateful for how I helped save her life.

"What did you think of the play" I asked Ski once we found ourselves alone in the car.

"It was *awesome!*" he answered.

I glanced over and read the expected sarcasm on his face.

"What did you love most about it?"

"First prize would have to go to the quality acting."

"And second?"

"To the entire stupid story."

"Why stupid?"

"Just that dopey old Don Quixote runs around making a fool of himself, getting beat up and humiliated constantly, and in the end accomplishes absolutely nothing, and now everyone thinks it's so inspiring. So he has an impossible dream – so what? It's all an illusion, it's pointless, it's meaningless.

"I've heard that some people in Spain treat *The Quixote* like their Bible," he continued. "What a ridiculous role model! I'd understand it if you were some college dropout frat boy who would like nothing better than to run around the country starting pointless fights, but...." Ski glanced over at me then. "Did *you* like it?" he asked.

"Yeah," I shrugged.

Ski just stared for a moment. "You're kidding, right?"

I didn't answer and Ski let it drop. "When are we going snowmobiling?"

"Probably Saturday."

"You're right," Ski said after a moment. "It was a good play."

I half smiled, wondering what would come next.

The Perfect Gift

"And way ahead of its time, too. Like trash TV centuries before electricity! We get to laugh at fools and feel better about our own shortcomings, which pale in comparison. I'm certain Cervantes would have made an excellent stand-up comedian if he were alive today."

23 Shortcuts

At home, we found three homemade pies and vanilla ice cream set on the kitchen table. Ski and I walked in and draped our coats over our chairs before sitting down and reaching for plates, forks, and dessert.

"How did you two like the play?" Grandma asked.

"It was *awesome*," Ski answered before I could say anything.

"What did you like best?" Grandma asked. This time Ski was stumped. He couldn't answer as sarcastically as he had to me.

"Uh," he stalled, thinking as quickly as he could. "There wasn't much point to his life," he began, "But at least he lived according to his convictions, crazy as they were."

"You thought there was no point to his life?" Grandma asked.

Ski just stared back, wondering what her point could possibly be. "Well," he began, then spoke slowly. "I'm not sure what it would be...."

"What about Dulcinea?" she probed. "Wouldn't *she* say there was a point to his life?"

"I guess so. Seems crazy that he'd go through all that trouble just to raise one tavern girl's self-esteem, though."

"What about himself?" Grandma continued.

"He was totally nuts. I don't think we can count delusions as a valid purpose to life."

"What if you look at his life metaphorically?"

"Are you saying we all have our own delusions to waste our lives on but believe they're worthwhile anyway?"

"I'm thinking we all have our lofty ideals and we often get beat up when we follow them, but if we never give up, then we'll win eventually; and if we give up and settle for less than our dreams...well, what kind of existence would that be?"

"I see your point," Ski conceded, though if I had the said the same thing, he'd have continued to argue, and I felt certain that he wasn't convinced. But he opted to avoid further confrontation and instead asked, "What are *your* lofty ideals?"

"Oh," Grandma said pensively, then leaned back in her chair and smiled broadly. Tears sprung into her eyes and for a moment, she couldn't speak. When she finally did, her voice broke. "Raising a good, loving family," she said, motioning around the room with one hand as others wandered in and took their seats. "And look!"

Ski nodded, looking around but only making eye contact with me. "Well done, Doña Quixote." I wondered whether Grandma's evidence, pointing out the entire family like "Exhibit A" in a trial, had successfully persuaded Ski to take her opinion more seriously.

Jim and Kellie walked inside holding hands. Kellie went to the fridge and pulled out a carton of eggnog while Jim went for glasses and set them around the table.

"How'd you all like the play?" Jim asked.

"It was awesome!" Ski exclaimed again, and I wondered if the same discussion would replay for the third time.

"Grandma," Ski asked somewhat pensively, "what would you say is the purpose of *my* life?"

"Well I don't know, Ski," she answered. "I suppose it could be just about anything you want it to be. But at the most basic level, it's the same as anyone else's."

"And what's that?"

"To experience joys and trials, to grow and learn, and to be happy."

"And how do you do that?" Ski asked. His face displayed a mixture of curiosity and skepticism.

"Sometimes you work hard, sometimes you just endure. Sometimes you take a break. But even then, you never forget your core values and goals. In the end, you come out a stronger, wiser, more capable and complete person."

"What if I don't want to wait till the end? I was kind of hoping to experience some happiness *before* I die."

"Ah," said Grandma knowingly, "you want the shortcuts."

Ski waited expectantly with one eyebrow raised. "What shortcuts?" he finally asked.

"Don't wait for life to beat you over the head with its lessons. Go out and learn them yourself."

Ski waited for a moment again before asking, "Where do you find them?"

"All around you," Grandma answered.

The Perfect Gift

Ski sighed and settled back in his chair when Grandma didn't continue, but he didn't look frustrated. He recognized her tactics. She was making him figure things out on his own the same way he always did to me. He glanced around the table, looking for clues.

"For example?" Ski finally asked.

"Anything that teaches you love, for example," Grandma answered.

"Like watching romantic chick flicks?" Ski asked. "Or eating cookies? I *do* love cookies. I could even get myself a cute little puppy with big, brown, irresistible eyes."

Grandma ignored Ski's sarcasm and Ski tried again. "Like meeting someone I'm interested in and spending time together and developing a relationship?"

"Yes, that's one type of love, but not the only one. There's also the kind of love you can feel for everyone. Unconditional love."

"I've heard of that, of course," Ski responded, "but I thought that was just an ideal, something to strive for but not necessarily achieve. Are you saying I could love *everyone*, even total strangers?"

"Yes," Grandma affirmed. "Even strangers."

"Hm," Ski responded. "How do you learn that? I'd be perfectly happy to walk through crowds and hug everyone and whisper sweet nothings in their ears, but I'm afraid they'd lock me up."

"Little things as much as anything," Grandma explained. "Doing service, showing kindness, focusing on someone other than yourself. You can't help feeling its effects on your heart, and after a while your mind catches up and understands, too. You begin to understand that it doesn't cost a cent to forgive, and an hour spent helping someone else becomes more valuable than most other ways we spend our time. Eventually you come to understand that love is an unlimited resource and that giving it away only brings you back more in return."

Ski nodded his head, thought for a moment, then sat up straighter in his chair and looked around the table, signaling that he had no further questions. I imagined him sitting down in a courtroom and declaring, "The prosecution rests."

I suddenly realized that this was the first serious conversation I had ever heard Ski participate in. He had all the necessary skills – asking important questions, injecting his personality to keep things interesting; he merely had to change his approach from sarcastic to sincere.

"We'll have to take you with us to more plays," Jim said after a prolonged silence. "That's the most interesting conversation I've heard for quite some time."

"Whatever happened between you and Netta?" Jim asked a few minutes later after the group had broken into several separate conversations.

"Things just didn't work out." I said. "You have to learn to let go of the past, I've learned that."

"Well, that's a good lesson" Jim admitted. "But you can learn more than one lesson from any experience, ya know."

"Do you have some other lesson in mind for me, or are you just philosophizing?"

Jim paused then, taking his time as was his nature. It made him impossible to argue with. Any argument would suffocate in the vacuum of silence before it could ever begin. "I have an idea of another lesson," he finally said. "I was just wondering if you ever gave her a real chance."

"How could I?" I answered. "She stopped writing. No matter how many messages I sent, she never wrote back. Not for months. I tried to call and she never answered. Maybe I didn't do everything perfectly, but it was the best I knew how - what more is there?"

"She didn't write?" Jim looked surprised.

"Not since last spring."

Jim processed that for another long moment, then asked, "Did you ever think of flying over there to talk things over and work things out?"

I thought about it plenty At first,. But it seemed ridiculous when she didn't even respond to my messages. And pointless. "By the time I realized that maybe I should, it was too late."

"Why too late?"

"Because she already hadn't written for months. That's a pretty clear statement of what she wanted, I'd say. I had no right to barge in on her life. And Julie and I had started dating, anyway. It didn't seem right to just run off to see an old girlfriend."

Jim paused again silently. I waited patiently for whatever he would say next. "When Kellie and I first met," he began, then paused again as if waiting for the second half of the sentence to be delivered to his mouth, "it seemed hopeless, too. She lived far away, had three years of school left, and I had nothing going for me financially." Jim watched the table top as he spoke, pausing frequently between words. "But I didn't give up. I looked around and made things happen and she joined in. We didn't know how to fit each other into our own worlds, so we found somewhere we could both fit in. I think of it as us choosing our own lives, because otherwise I might never get what I want. Sometimes I still can't believe it's all working out, but it is."

He paused again, then looked up and clasped his hands together on the table. "I don't know about you two. That's just how it worked out for us. I think it worked out because I finally figured out exactly what I wanted, and it was Kellie. Once I had that clear, I found a way to make everything else possible." Kellie reached up and folded one of her hands around his. Jim looked me in the eye and smiled amicably. "I hope I don't sound like I'm lecturing you."

"That's a great story, Jim," I said. "I'm glad things worked out so well for the two of you. Julie and I were lucky—we're both graduating soon and I'm sure we'll both find jobs near each other. Things are falling right into place."

"And do you know exactly what you want?" Jim asked.

"Yeah, I think I do." I caught myself feeling the slightest bit defensive, as if Jim thought I was wrong.

"Well, I suppose you would know what's best for you better than me," Jim confessed. "I just know one thing about Netta."

"What's that?" I asked casually, hiding my curiosity.

"That she was different with you than I had ever seen her before. She just glowed," he said matter-of-factly. "She was totally in love with you."

Rather than make me feel good, this information brought up the old resentment and confusion. "She sure had a nice way of showing it."

"Well, things did change after she left for France. At first, she talked about not even going, about maybe moving to Logan to be near you. She regretted not letting herself like you earlier, but felt lucky that you held on and didn't give up on her. Then last summer she said you seemed distant, but I figured you two would work that out."

Now I knew more of the story and it made me feel sad. Not that things didn't work out, necessarily. We couldn't have lasted for three years apart anyway. I felt sad that things had turned sour rather than ending on better terms.

If only we could have stayed in touch, maybe everything would have turned out better. Then again, maybe not. I had no way of knowing now.

"I'm surprised to hear that she stopped writing," Jim added, "because every once in a while she mentioned what you had been doing."

"Really?" I asked. At least I knew she was reading the messages I sent. It made me curious what she said about me.

"How often do you hear from her?" I asked.

"Every month or two. Less often lately."

"How's she doing?"

"Good," Jim merely answered. "Doing pretty good."

"Well, I appreciate the information, Jim," I said, "even if it doesn't matter anymore."

Jim raised one eyebrow. "It doesn't matter?" he asked, perplexed.

"No." I didn't know why it would. "Julie's better for me anyway. She's about as smart as Netta, even more beautiful, and she would never give up on me. So I can trust her. I know we could work anything out together. That's important to me."

"But Spencer," Kellie began, "do you love her as much?"

"Sure," I answered. "It's different, but good. It's the kind that grows, too, not just infatuation, ya know?"

"Are you saying you were only infatuated with Annetta?" Kellie asked.

"I don't know, there may have been more than just that. But it's over now and I have Julie, so why should I worry about it?"

"But Spencer," Kellie said slowly, looking me in the eye, "If you two had something special, then maybe you still could." She looked at me as if wondering if her point was getting through to me at all.

"Oh, yeah," I assured her, "I know what you're saying. Don't worry about me. I know what I'm doing."

Kellie took a breath and opened her mouth to say something more, but Jim squeezed her hand and she stopped.

I went to take another bite of pumpkin pie and found my plate empty. I reached out and dished myself a slice as Kellie passed me the ice cream.

"I should go," Jim told Kellie. "I have to get up early."

"Early, Jim?" Grandma asked from the other end of the table where she and Ski had been talking. "I'm not sure I've ever heard you use that word. What time would you consider early?"

Jim grinned. "Four a.m."

"That's not early," Ski disagreed. "That's *late.*"

"One end of Mark Cherrington's barn roof collapsed with the last storm. I promised I'd help him fix it, and that's my only free time before I have to get to work," Jim reported.

The Perfect Gift

"That's very kind of you," Grandma said. Jim accepted the compliment with a slight nod and stood up to go.

Kellie walked him outside to his truck and the rest of us stared at the table and our empty plates, also considering calling it a night. A minute later, Kellie walked back inside and closed the door, shivering but grinning from ear to ear. She stood in the kitchen doorway for a moment, her eyes resting on the table but her thoughts far away, then apparently deciding nothing here could top the goodnight kiss, said "Goodnight," and turned to walk dreamily upstairs.

Just then Ski jumped up from his chair and rushed past her, startling everyone in the room. He turned and ran outside without his coat, not even bothering to shut the door behind him.

We all exchanged curious glances and I walked over and shut the door. Everyone else stood then, wished each other good night, scooted their chairs under the table and made their way upstairs.

I had just crawled under the heavy blankets on my bed, enjoying the momentary cold of the sheets, when Ski stepped into the room.

"Do you have an alarm clock?" he asked. I pointed to the rolltop desk against one wall and he found an old clock, wound it, and set the alarm. What felt like five minutes later, the raucous alarm woke me with a start and Ski rolled over and shut it off. The room was dark.

"What time is it?" I asked Ski in a husky voice.

"Four," he answered, climbing out of bed and pulling his clothes on.

"What are you doing?"

"Helping fix Mark's barn."

I considered that for a moment, still half asleep and fading away quickly. "Why?"

Ski pulled on his coat, then stopped and stood in the middle of the dark room. "Because I got thinking. Maybe Don Quixote had something up on me. He had no brain to speak of, but he lived with heart and maybe that means he lived more fully. So I thought I should at least give it a try."

"Hmm," I merely grunted.

"And what better way to prove my insanity," Ski continued, "than by waking up in the middle of the night in the middle of winter in the middle of nowhere to help someone I've never met and will never see again?"

"You don't waste any time, do you?"

"You're the one who's supposed to know about these things. If you believe what your Grandmother says about service and happiness and all, I don't know why you're not rolling out of bed, too."

"Are you saying that *you* believe her?"

"It's worth a try. This is study abroad, remember? I'm going native!"

A faint light appeared outside and the sound of Jim's truck engine and tires crunching over the snow filtered in. I began to consider whether to get dressed and join Ski on his little experiment.

"Gotta go," Ski announced. I fell asleep before the back door shut behind him.

24 Missing Pieces

Ski had returned home and fallen asleep before I woke up at nine. French toast and scrambled eggs were still warm in the oven when I wandered downstairs for a late breakfast, and Grandma walked into the kitchen as I ate. "Jim left something for you," she said, then set a glass in the sink and left.

I shoved another bite of syrup-dripping toast into my mouth and turned toward the counter where Grandma had indicated. A green shoe box sat there alone. I turned back to the table and finished eating before setting my plate in the sink and picking up the box. When I removed the top, I found a stack of a dozen old letters. The unfamiliar stamps and blue *par avion* stickers identified them immediately. I picked them up and found Annetta's and Amy's names written in the upper left corners of the envelopes above a return address in Marseilles.

I stared at them for a moment before putting them back in the shoe box and carrying them up to my room. I wanted to read these alone. After all the months of wondering what Annetta was up to, I would finally find out.

Ski never stirred as I sat down in the antique overstuffed chair near my bed and sorted through the letters to find the oldest postmark. For a moment I doubted if I should really be reading Jim's letters or not, but he had brought them for just that purpose. There couldn't be any harm in it.

From February 12:

Dear Jim,

It feels so wonderful to be back in a city! There are people everywhere, and I love to just walk through the crowds. Sometimes people talk to me, trying to sell me things, I suppose, and I have no idea what they're saying so I just smile and shrug my shoulders and keep on walking.

But there are times when I also miss the quiet and solitude of the Amber Valley. Sometimes I wake up in my small white-washed room and wish I could walk out into the center of a snowy field and lay down in the snow and stare at the big, blue sky and do nothing else all day long. When night fell I would watch the stars fall.

Lucky for me, the beach isn't far from home. The Mediterranean is so different from the Pacific. It's so calm, but also beautiful. You'd be amazed at how blue it is some days. It's gorgeous. If it was warmer, I'd stay all afternoon, but at least in February I have it pretty well to myself....

I finished the first letter and slid the second from its envelope.

March 4:

Dear Jim,

I found a new favorite place today. I got lost while looking for a friend's house (Elodie's, who I told you about in the last letter) ...

The first letter I read said nothing about Elodie. I picked up the pile of envelopes again and looked for the missing letter, but found no postmarks between these first two letters. I guess Jim didn't give me all of them to read.

...I was wandering through thin, narrow streets near the old city center when I came upon a small square with a fountain in the center. Everything there was still and quiet, away from traffic sounds. The fountain wasn't running and the water at the base was very still, reflecting the buildings and balconies and blue sky. I took a franc from my pocket and threw it in and made a wish, even, then sat there and just thought (just *reflected*, I should say!) for at least half an hour. I felt so refreshed afterward!

How is everyone and everything in Amber? How are *you* doing? You sounded restless in your last letter. Do you want to call me sometime? My number here is....

I finished another letter and began reading the fourth.
April 21:

Dear Jim,
    It was so nice to hear your voice this morning! What a sweet surprise!
But you're right, it's not the same when we can't see each other, so I'm
sending you these pictures...

I dropped the letter and picked up the envelope again,
squeezing it to look in, and sure enough, three photos had been
shoved deep inside. I poured them out into my hand and held them
all up together.
    The first showed Annetta sitting at a small cement fountain
in a shady courtyard. She had one leg crossed over the other as
she leaned back on one arm. Her hair had grown longer. Her face
was just as tan, her eyes as green. One of her hands was resting
somewhat awkwardly on her knee, and as I peered closer, I saw a
gold-looking coin held between her fingers.
    I wondered what she was wishing for now.
    The second picture showed Netta sitting calmly in the sand,
her legs crossed, wind blowing her light brown hair away from her
face, and wearing a light jacket. A thin strip of sky was on fire as the
sun rose over the beach and sea in the background. At one edge of
the photo stood Amy, leaning awkwardly into the picture, making a
face and laughing.
    The third picture showed the entire family standing, arms
wrapped loosely around each other's shoulders and waists, eyes
squinting into the sun, in front of what must have been their home.
    I gazed at the pictures a while longer, then went back to
reading.

Sorry about not telling you what I wished for! I'm pretty sure if you tell
anyone your wish, it won't come true ...

Near the end of August, Amy wrote a letter.

Jimmy!
    Yahoo! You go, boy! You're in love! I can tell! Don't try denying
it! I am so excited for you. She sounds awesome. And don't worry,

The Perfect Gift

things will work out. You'll figure out something.

Anyway, why are you talking about finding a good enough job in Amber? Move away! Go west! Even if you love it there, don't expect her to. Find somewhere bigger where you can both find more things to fill your lives with. Don't you think?

Gosh, I sound like Netta all of a sudden! Telling people what to do and bossing you around! I'm sorry. I am <u>so</u> sorry! It will <u>never</u> happen again!

Listen, I'm sending you a poem I wrote this spring. It's called "The Darkest Hour." If you ever get discouraged about Kellie, just read this!! It's a sure thing to cheer you up, and if it doesn't cheer you up, then just remember who sent it to ya and <u>that</u> can not fail to make you smile!

I checked the envelope for the poem, but found nothing.

The next letter came from Netta and told about their summer vacation to Spain. Inside the envelope was another photo, this time of Netta and Amy standing in the open doorway of some kind of ancient castle with the blue, blue Mediterranean shimmering far below. Netta's face had tanned dark, her hair had grown even longer, and her green eyes sparkled brightly in the sun. She looked more beautiful than ever. On the back of the picture was written "Aguilas, August 13. Spain is beautiful but too hot!"

I flipped the picture back over and stared at Netta, so slender and tan and flashing that dazzling smile. I left the photo on my knee and continued to read.

September 12:

...I called it off with Jean Michael. He was shocked, then angry, then hurt, but I just couldn't see him anymore. It didn't feel...right, ya know? He's the nicest guy I've met over here and he's always been really good to me and I tell him that and he shrugs one shoulder and makes a little *pfff* sound through his lips and asks "Alors, qu'est-ce qui se passe?" —what's up then? But I still can't explain it to him. But I'll tell you, if he tries to hug and kiss me one more time, I'll put it very clearly for him! Just because I can't answer all his questions doesn't mean I'm wrong or don't know what I want!

I felt a pang of jealousy leap into my heart as I read the letter, but quickly pushed it away. How ridiculous. I had no right or reason. The next paragraph took me completely by surprise.

Maybe I'll break down and tell him about Spencer. It would be easy then to explain why I don't want to keep dating him if I could explain why I knew we'd never be everything I have learned to hope for, but what good would that do? I don't believe he really wants to hear that.

Speaking of Spencer, I haven't heard from him for a while now. He must be busy in school. I miss his letters. It's nice, sometimes, to remember some of my last month back home. He's so unique, isn't he?

Congratulations about Kellie! I am so happy for you two! Keep me posted on all future developments!

I let the letter and my hand drop to my knee. Had I read right? Now I knew she read my messages and said she enjoyed them, but still never wrote back! I didn't understand what she could have been thinking.

I also knew that I still meant something to her, but what? It didn't matter, I reminded myself, but it still felt nice to know.

September 29:

I got the teaching job and I love it! The children are _so_ adorable! Jean Luc doesn't say much with his mouth but his eyes speak volumes. He loves me and follows me everywhere!

Julie (I call her Juliette) is so creative and energetic, always drawing from her imagination and babbling on and on about everything. The other teachers get exasperated by her, but if I ask her to sit quietly, she folds her fingers together and just sits and watches me—at least for a minute or two.

Nathalie's the cutest. So adorable. Sweet and independent. I'll have to send you a picture sometime. Sometimes I feel like I'm looking back eighteen years into the past and seeing myself in her eyes.

That, in turn, makes me reflect on everything I've been through since I was such a little girl, and it feels kind of bittersweet to admit that some of that simple innocence can never be regained.

It's always hard to let things go, even when there's absolutely nothing you can do about it.

Now I remembered clearly what I liked best about Annetta. It was both the way she saw the world—all the beauty and life in it—and her ability to participate in it, to engage, even when only a spectator, by feeling it so deeply.

When we were together, when I looked into her eyes, she made me feel the same way. She made life feel sweet and worth living. And if she made me feel like no one else ever had, then what if....

Ski woke up and rolled slowly over to stare out the window with half-open eyelids.

"So, did it work?" I asked him.

"Of course it worked."

"Wow! How does it feel?"

Ski sat up on the side of his bed and crunched up his nose at me. "What are you talking about?" he asked, beginning to yawn.

"You know. The service. The happiness."

"Oh, that," Ski said blandly, beginning a stretch. "No, it was too cold to feel good out there. Happiness freezes and shatters at about fifteen below zero."

"Then what did you say worked?"

"The roof," Ski answered, looking at me as if I was stupid. "The roof worked. It stayed up. That means it worked, right?" I nodded once. "If I don't hurry," he mumbled, scuffling slowly out of the room in bare feet, "I'll be late for breakfast."

Maybe I *was* stupid. Not because of anything Ski could say, but because of what I had begun to think and feel. I had begun to miss Netta. I wished she could be here, if only so I could look into her eyes and answer the question I began to ask myself for the first time since last summer: What if?

25 Closure

I put down the last letter fifteen minutes later. My heart thudded in my throat. I felt wonderful and conflicted all mixed together. It came out as a restlessness churning against the insides of my ribs and skull. I had to get outside and clear my head.

The cold air outside helped a little, but a few of my young cousins who had been building lop-sided snowmen waved and began tromping toward me in their over-sized snow boots. I didn't want to play with them until I had relaxed a little, so I waved back and climbed into the truck.

I headed down the highway toward town with no plan other than to drive until I felt like turning around.

Because Netta never wrote back, I had never had the chance to get closure, to completely finish that chapter of my life. I had simply made assumptions and learned to live with them. Now my mind was filled with new information and questions and it would take a minute to let the puzzle pieces fall back into place inside my mind and let everything make sense again.

I glanced down at the speedometer and found it pegged at 85 mph. I shifted into neutral and the truck rolled half a mile before coming to a stop on top of a small hill. I coasted off the side of the road and turned off the key, then leaned forward, draping my arms around the steering wheel.

Nothing moved. Everything turned silent except my own breathing. I sighed and slumped more heavily forward, letting my chin rest on my forearm, staring out through the windshield. My eyes slipped slowly over the horizon of smoothly sloped foothills and distant mountain summits, which I hadn't taken time to stare at for many years.

As a child living in Amber for the summer, I would climb trees or get up on top of cars or into the barn's loft, anywhere I could go that offered an uninterrupted view of the horizon.

I thought if I could memorize the boundaries of my world, then I would never get lost. If I knew all the shapes of the surrounding hills and mountains, then I could always look up and know exactly where I stood and how to find my way home.

The memory made me half-way smile. I remembered sitting sometimes for hours and tracing the horizon with my eyes, then closing them and retracing the contours again in my mind.

I remembered waking up after having fallen asleep there in the sun, a new touch of rosy pink sunburn on my already dark skin. I remembered feeling secure within the boundaries of my limited little world. The simplicity lent the days a happy, carefree atmosphere that I have longed for ever since. The fact that I can never go back to the simplicity of youth gave the memories a tangy, bittersweet taste inside my heart.

The problem, as I began to range farther and farther from the house and barn, was that everything looked different from different angles. How could I ever hope to recognize every shape of every side of every hill? The farther I went from home, the smaller my chances of always knowing where I was and where I was going.

And my destinations changed as well. No longer could I simply return home at the end of each day, climb into bed and dream until Grandpa woke me to help milk the cows. Now my destinations waited somewhere out in the grand, unexplored, uncharted world of the future. The familiar horizon could tell me where I've been and where I am now, that's all. It can't tell me where to go next.

I closed my eyes and let my mind drift through the past, watching the images of bright, clear summer mornings spent running through the tall rows of corn and wheat growing higher than my head, fuzzy memories flickering against the back of my eyelids like an old home movie. I listened for the lazy buzz of flies in the silent heat of endless summer afternoons and muggy, mosquito-filled evenings cleaning the barn.

I remembered as I began growing up. Once I had my driver's license I no longer spent summers here, but each time I came to visit, each time I pulled off the highway and into Amber and into Grandma's driveway, everything still felt magic. The valley still felt sweet and warm and welcoming. I still felt loved and happy and secure.

I remembered the waitress I met here last Christmas and fell quickly in love with—if that's what it was. I could never explain what it was about Annetta that brought us so close to each other so quickly. I only knew the way I felt when we spent time together. I only knew how everything she said seemed to matter so much. How she made me feel so alive. How I loved to hear her talk and watch her green eyes flash with passion and intelligence and depth and, later, love.

As the memories returned, so did the inner tension. I started the truck again and drove on toward town and the highway. I turned left at the bridge and considered driving past the Hall's old house, but thought better of it and drove to the library instead.

Of course! That's exactly what I needed! Some reading to take my mind off all my current thoughts and feelings. Even a momentary escape would make things that much better when I closed the book again.

The building looked deserted as I opened the heavy door and stepped inside. I crossed the wood floor, listening to the familiar squeak of the boards, then wandered through the shelves and took down a few books that caught my attention.

I carried the books to the back room where Netta and I used to read and talk. At first, I doubted the wisdom of staying in this place that might bring back even more troubling memories, but a few pages of the first book put me beyond danger, out of reach of my present surroundings.

Shaun Roundy

I finished three chapters of the book and was feeling much better when I realized that I was reading the sequel to some other story. Everything would make much more sense if I started at the beginning. I set the book down and walked toward the card catalogue to find the first book.

As I passed by the circulation desk, a floor board creaked loudly underfoot and a head covered with wild gray hair popped up from behind the desk and startled me. He looked as if he had been sleeping.

"Well, hello, Jared. It is good to see you again!"

It was Mr. Milligan, the librarian. He was a friend of Grandma's and I knew him from when he used to bring by library books for me to read in the summers when I was a child and couldn't drive to the library myself. He always seemed to know exactly which books a ten-year-old child would enjoy. He was kind and thoughtful even if his memory for names wasn't the best. Jared was my cousin.

"Actually, I'm Spencer," I answered, "and it's good to see you, too."

"Oh, do forgive me. I can never keep all of your names straight, but I do remember that you are the one attending school in Utah. How is that treating you, may I ask?"

Mr. Milligan's grammar was always perfect, as if he washed and ironed it every morning.

"Really well," I answered. "At least, I can say that now that finals are over."

"Well I am certainly pleased to hear that. Did you drive up alone this year?"

"Nope," I answered, then felt an urge to apologize for using any form of slang in his presence. "I brought my roommate."

"Wonderful. I shall look forward to meeting him. It will be a treat."

"Oh, you won't forget it. He's quite a character."

"And why are you bringing home a roommate instead of a young lady?" Mr. Milligan's green eyes twinkled as he began to pry.

"Ah, you know how it goes," I answered, dodging the question.

"Yes," he answered. "It must be difficult when she is far away in France."

Of course he was talking about Annetta. He wouldn't know that we weren't a thing anymore. I almost resented his reminding me of what I had come here to forget. "Yeah," I agreed. There was

The Perfect Gift

no point explaining the entire situation. Someone would eventually find out and gossip would spread through the small community quickly enough.

"But does absence not make the heart grow fonder?" Mr. Milligan asked. I just nodded my head. "And would you not enjoy communicating with her?"

I nodded my head again. What was he getting at?

"Well I have always said that there is no time like the present to accomplish an important task. Let me get you some paper and a cup of hot cocoa. You can write to your lovely damsel while you warm yourself before stepping back into the cold."

The silence of the library, broken only by the distant hum of an ancient furnace, was pleasant; and Mr. Milligan's offer of hot cocoa sounded especially nice, so I humored both of us by accepting.

He handed me a sheet of the library's simple letterhead and a short, eraser-free number two pencil and I made my way to a table near the card catalogue. I sat down and wondered which of "my lovely damsels" I should write to. When Mr. Milligan appeared with a styrofoam cup of hot chocolate and an envelope addressed to France, I saw that the decision had been made for me.

Dear Annetta,
Hi. How's France?

That was a dumb question. Ah, well, what does it matter?

I just got in to Amber a couple days ago. It hasn't changed much since you left.

That wasn't entirely true. Without her around, the town wasn't nearly as interesting.

So how are things? What's new in your life?

For a moment I considered asking if she still wasn't talking to Jean Michael or if she had made any wishes in her fountain lately, but decided against it. Better to take the safe route for now and not risk getting her mad at Jim for sharing his letters, or at me for reading them.

Shaun Roundy

Is France turning out to be everything you expected?

How ridiculous. Here I was trying to act as if everything was fine and normal. Asking questions as if she would ever answer them. I wanted to talk with her and relax and clarify everything once and for all and get over her and get on with life, but what's the point of writing anything at all if she never writes back?

No, I wouldn't send her a letter, at least not without something better to say. I'd wait till I got everything straightened out in my heart and mind, at least, then maybe I'd write, just to let her know that I was happy, that I was over her, and that my life was moving along fine without her.

For now, I'd just use this page to scribble out my thoughts. I'd use it to sort out the feelings I thought I had forgotten. That couldn't hurt anything.

Things are going great with me. They're going really well with Julie. We're getting pretty serious. Maybe really serious. I'll know for sure after the break. But there's one thing that bothers me now. Since I've been back in Amber, I've begun remembering how it felt to be around you. I've been remembering what a neat girl you are. I've never met anyone else quite like you. I just don't know what all that means. Julie is smart and fun and beautiful and we get along great and I love her. I just wish I could know that I would never regret not getting to know you once more to find out if we would have a chance together and if we'd want to take that chance.

This was working well! The words and ideas I wrote surprised me but they helped me discover and clarify the feelings and questions filling my mind and heart.

Here's what I wish I could ask you—did you feel the same thing about me? Was there really something special between us? Did I complete or compliment you in a way you had never experienced before? Or was it just a nice, romantic, but temporary fling? Would it have lasted if we hadn't been so far apart? I know it doesn't much matter since you're on the other side of the world for two more years and you don't seem to care anyway and I've mostly forgotten you by now.

The simple truth is that all of a sudden I can't stop thinking about you. I wish you were here. I miss you. Even though we'd never get back together, I would like nothing better than to see and talk with you again.

It's so funny! When you didn't answer my letters, I used to force myself to forget about you. Since I got back to Amber, I've allowed myself to remember again and on one hand, it's the nicest possible thing. On the other, it brings back some of the old frustrations and questions....

Regardless of all that, I still think I'm going to marry Julie. She's such a terrific girl. Maybe you were even better for me in some ways, but if we always waited for the best thing, we'd never get anything done, would we? Life goes on and leaves us behind if we don't go along with it.

Writing as if I was explaining things to Netta forced me to finish one thought before my mind jumped on to the next question. But it made me far too open to ever really send the letter. It made me sound like I understood the questions and answers better than I really did. But writing brought me closer to understanding, so I continued.

It seems funny that I'm writing all these things to you. I'm sure you're wondering when I'll get a clue and get over you. Don't worry about me! Even if I still have a few questions, I've accepted the way things are and have given up on us. I just wish I could know for sure what that was between us last year and why you never wrote me back. It would be nice to know that, to never have to wonder about you again, ya know? That would be nice.

At that point, I ran out of things to say. I had outlined all my questions. Even if I had no way of answering them fully, at least I knew exactly what questions I was dealing with. It was time to close the letter.

> By the way, if there was anything I did or didn't do that bothered or hurt you, I'm sorry. I'm sure I didn't handle everything perfectly. I was trying to do the best I knew how, but our best isn't always good enough, is it? It just seems crazy that we didn't at least stay friends and stay in touch.
> Merry Christmas. Say hi to Amy and your dad.

I deliberated for a moment over the next line, then finally wrote:

> Love,
> Spence

That was about as much as I was going to learn from this little exercise. Nothing further could be learned by talking to myself. I folded the letter and stuffed it into the envelope. Now it was time to live in the present again.

I needed to get moving and let myself forget about these unanswerable questions. I needed to get home and lose myself by talking and playing with all my relatives there.

I drained the cup of hot chocolate and walked toward the front door. Mr. Milligan wasn't at the circulation desk, so I tossed the envelope and my cup into the garbage can next to his chair. "Thanks, Mr. Milligan!" I shouted.

"Nice to see you again, Jared!" Mr. Milligan shouted from somewhere behind the rows of books.

"You, too," I shouted back, then walked out the door.

26 Santa Claus is Coming to Town

I had calmed down and felt better by the time I pulled into the driveway at home. Sorting out my thoughts had helped. It had become clear to me once more that entertaining any questions about

Annetta was pointless. I knew what I was doing. Everything was great just the way it was.

In the front yard, I found Ski and some of the kids surrounding a cluster of very creative snow sculptures. I examined a unicorn, a castle, and a horse pulling a sleigh.

I climbed out of the car and watched for a few minutes. Ski really seemed to be enjoying himself, and all the kids vied for his attention.

"Ski," said Saedi, a shy four-year old cousin, taking his gloved hand and bending her head far back to look up at his face. "Can I ride your horsey?"

Ski reached down and picked her up. He hoisted her high into the air, Saedi grinning from ear to ear, before setting her down on the horse's back.

"Giddy up," she said quietly, then smiled happily at Ski.

"I want to ride! I want to ride!" the other kids shouted, crowding around Ski in an effort to be noticed first.

"You can't *all* ride," Ski explained, reaching around to muss their hair. "Old Bessie's back isn't strong enough to hold all of you at once."

I was surprised to see that this answer satisfied them. They seemed content just having his undivided attention. I was surprised to realize that the children loved him. Then Ski grinned a mischievous smile.

"Ah, what the heck," he said. "You're all so small, Old Bessie probably won't even know you're there." He started lifting the kids and setting them behind Saedi until the snow horse suddenly crumbled beneath their weight and they all tumbled to the ground in a writhing, giggling mass.

"Looks like fun," I commented as Ski left the yard and walked toward me.

"Hey, at least it got me away from the grownups and their constant questions," he explained.

Saedi followed us as we walked around the house and in the back door to find Alisha and Diane beginning a game of Scrabble next to a near-empty plate of homemade donuts and a half-eaten pumpkin pie.

"Can we play?" I asked.

"Sure," Alisha answered. "Spencer, you be on Saedi's team," she dictated, "and Ski...."

"Ski's on my team!" Diane shouted quickly, cutting her off mid-sentence.

Shaun Roundy

During the first half of the game I noticed Ski watching Diane and listening closely to her little stories, letting her figure out and choose the words, only helping a little here and there. "We make a good team," Diane told him.

I could tell he was busy learning what it meant to connect with someone, to open up and trust and be genuine and vulnerable. Sometimes his eyes showed concentration as he traced a thought or observed a feeling. After a few moments he'd look up again, totally absorbed in the present moment, in the game at hand.

By the time the game pieces to draw from ran out, a few others had gathered around the table behind us, surveying our letters and watching the board. Alisha held a twelve point lead. Di and Ski put down "jumps" and had four letters left.

"Saedi," her older brother said, "you can put...."

"Hey!" Alisha warned, raising a finger toward him. "No cheating."

"Di," I said, "I'll give you a thousand dollars if you get me a glass of juice."

"Okay." She ran to the kitchen and returned with a tall glass of grape juice just as I was ready to spell my next word. "Now you owe me a hundred million billion dollars," she told me, estimating my tab after all the times I offered her a thousand dollars to do something for me. "You can pay me whenever you want."

"Thanks, Di," I said as Saedi and I laid down our pieces. "Thanks, using your s. That's 13 points, with a double word score gives us 26. We're winning!" Saedi held up her tiny hand for a high five.

"Nice one, Spencer," said Alisha, "but not nice enough. Using your T, I can spell Santa—5 points, with a triple word score makes 15. And that's the end of the game!"

"Sorry, you can't do that," I smiled. "*Santa*'s a proper noun."

"Uh-uh," Alisha argued, "it's not a proper name because he's not real."

"Uh-huh!" protested Diane. "He is too real!"

"No he's not, Di," Alisha shook her head. "Mary told me in second grade that Mom and Dad bring us the presents."

"So?" retorted Diane in her sauciest voice. "Mary doesn't know *everything*."

"Wanna hear about the time I met Santa?" asked Ski. Everyone turned to Ski and waited for the story, which he took as a 'yes.'

"My first Christmas after we moved to Washington, DC, I

was wandering around Georgetown and this big guy in a sleigh pulled by eight tiny reindeer landed right in front of me. He had all these boxes and stuff in the back of his sleigh, so I figured he was selling something. Anyway, I walked over to check out the merchandise.

"So he's sitting in the sleigh trying to unfold the biggest road map I've ever seen. When he sees me watching him, he asks, 'Excuse me, but can you tell me where to find the White House? I'd like to unload some coal before I get on with my rounds.'

"So I said, 'Sure! Ya just catch the Yellow Line over at...' and then I noticed he wouldn't be able to take the Metro with his sleigh and reindeer—the only animals you can have on the Metro are seeing-eye dogs. So he said, 'Why don't you hop in my sleigh and you can show me?'

"Well, I knew better than to accept rides from weirdos in the District, but this guy seemed harmless enough. He dressed all in red from his head to his toe and had a belly that shook when he laughed like a bowl full of Jell-o."

"Jelly!" Alisha and Saedi shouted in unison.

"Hey, who's telling the story—you guys or me?" The girls grinned and waited for Ski to continue.

"I hopped in the sleigh and we flew up over Key Bridge and down along the Potomac, then turned left at the Lincoln Memorial. It was pretty cool. Anyway, it didn't take me long to figure out that this was Santa Claus himself. I started trying to be good real quick by helping him unload the coal at the White House, and when he was dropping me off again in Georgetown, I asked if he had anything for me.

"He just looked at me and laughed, doing that Jell-o thing again, and told me that he only brought stuff to people who believe in him. I had sort of forgotten that I didn't. So if you don't believe in Santa, Ali, I guess he doesn't bring presents to *you*, but that doesn't mean that his name's not a proper noun. Find another word."

Ski was having more fun than I had ever seen and I watched in ongoing, pleasant surprise. He fluctuated between being guarded and open, even taking a few jabs at himself to try it out. Everyone went on talking and laughing as Alisha looked for another word to spell, and at one point I saw Ski laugh one laugh that came from deep down inside himself. He immediately stopped, startled at himself and, I suppose, the feeling that must have accompanied that genuine, mirthful laugh.

Alisha spelled "stand" instead and earned the triple word

score.

Suddenly everyone outside the immediate circle was speaking to play next. "Why don't you play another game with us," Uncle Jon asked Ski. "We haven't had much time to talk yet."

Ski's face went blank momentarily. He looked at Jon and the slightest bit of uneasiness showed in his expression. "Well," he finally answered, "I've been sitting down a bit too long. Think I'll go stretch my legs. Thanks, though."

Ski stood up and his chair filled quickly. He stretched and yawned a little, then nodded his head to one side as a signal for me to follow him, and walked casually toward the back door.

27 Progress

When I stepped out the door, Ski had already crossed the yard to the barn. We still hadn't unloaded the firewood from the back of the truck, and Ski swung the heavy barn door open wide, then started dragging logs from the truck bed and piling them against the wall..

"How am I doing?" he asked as I hopped into the truck bed to hand him logs.

"You look more relaxed," I told him, "and like you're enjoying yourself."

"I am," he agreed, "but I don't feel different. It's like I stretched my comfort zone a little, but I haven't really changed. I was expecting something to change."

"What gave you that idea?"

"ThAt first, day," he said, "when we had that talk at the hot springs. I felt different then. I thought it would continue, I hoped that would be a more permanent change."

"Maybe it was," I offered.

"Oh," Ski replied, "I thought you were listening to me, because I just said that I *don't* feel that way anymore, and I somehow got the idea that you heard me."

"What I mean is," I explained, "that you might have felt different when you changed because it was new. It was different. And maybe you're still different than you were, but now you've grown used to the new way, so it doesn't *feel* different anymore."

Ski thought about that as I handed him another armful of sawed logs. "I am a little different, aren't I? I just thought it would feel…well, okay, I'll be patient then. Right? Anyway, I'm sick of talking about myself. This whole vacation has become all about me. How could you let this happen?"

Ski's sarcastic accusation seemed like his normal self, but some of its edge had softened, as if the edge were now made of wood and not tempered steel. *That's progress*, I thought.

"So what about you?" Ski asked when he came for his next arm load. "How are you doing?"

"Fine," I answered. I hadn't thought of sharing any of my recent thoughts about missing Annetta with anyone, and part of me wanted to, but that might complicate things. I didn't know where to begin or what to say, and didn't want to start into an explanation I couldn't finish and get myself tangled into a knot of confusion. I'd figure it out on my own.

No, I wouldn't, I corrected myself. I wouldn't figure it out. Or rather, I already *had* figured it out. All I needed was time to get used to the new information I had acquired and let it all sink in. Once it did, it wouldn't change anything, except to perhaps provide a little more understanding about why Netta had never written.

Everything would work out, that's all I knew. It always does. It had to.

"Ya know," Ski mused, "I never really thought about wanting to change or even cared until this last summer."

I was still lost in my own thoughts and didn't pay much attention to Ski's words. I could tell from the tone of his voice that he was just thinking out loud anyway.

"And then I thought I could learn everything and change in one month, max."

I continued half-listening, half-following my own thoughts.

"But it didn't turn out that easy. Guess I just needed a little help."

Ski stopped carrying wood then and stared at me. "Are you even listening?"

I looked up from my thoughts. "Not really," I admitted.

"Doesn't matter," he shrugged. "I wasn't talking to you anyway."

28 Close Quarters

I woke up from a dream about Netta. It wasn't the angry, silent girl I had sensed in the forest glade or along the snowy gravel road. This time she ran, laughing as she went, through piles of bright red and yellow autumn leaves. Behind her stood a towering, snowcapped mountain. When she saw me staring up at the distant peak, she stopped laughing and stood still, a somber look falling across her face.

"It's not so far away," she said solemnly, pointing to the mountain. "I promise."

She walked slowly up to me then until she stood less than a foot from my chin. Her bright green eyes stared into mine questioningly, as if looking for something lost, wondering if it could be found in my eyes. She sighed once and smiled tiredly at me, and I awoke with the image of her freckled nose and beautiful eyes burned into my memory.

I knew the dream was only a result of my mind working overtime to sort everything out, but I held onto the pleasant image for as long as I could anyway, lying in bed and staring up at the whitewashed ceiling.

Remembering this sweet side of Annetta felt good, I had to admit. There was no use lying to myself or ignoring the truth. It didn't change anything, but I complimented myself on having come to terms with that fact, at least. I no longer had to force myself to avoid thinking about her and our past.

Then I turned my thoughts to Julie. Julie was my future. Julie would continue to bring me happiness while my memory of Annetta would fade. As I thought of Julie, I began to feel alarmed that the image of her face was dimmer than my recent dream image of Annetta. I focused more carefully, remembering her bright blue eyes, perfect smile, clear skin, her arms around my neck, her face drawing near mine…

"Spencer!" Alisha shouted through the door, tapping it a few times with her knuckles. "Phone!"

I got up and walked downstairs to the living room which had already begun to fill with family who had just finished their breakfast.

"Hello?" I said into the receiver, talking over the sound of the piano playing Scott Joplin's *Maple Leaf Rag* in the living room, wondering who might have called.

"Spencer!" Julie's voice shouted across the line.

"Hi!" I answered enthusiastically. "How are you?"

"What do *you* think?" Julie teased.

"Perfect," I answered, my standard but honest response to that question. In the back of my mind, I thought of Andrea, the local telephone operator on the town's party line, hearing every word, eager to repeat the story to anyone with a listening ear. Amber was too small and too remote to have any cell service, or I'd have spent every evening talking to Julie. At least I wouldn't have to explain anything to Mr. Milligan now about Annetta.

"Well, the truth is," Julie continued, "I'm not quite perfect."

"I highly doubt that," I argued.

"I'm just missing my favorite person is all."

"Oh, yeah?" I asked, "and who would that be?"

"Ski, silly – who did you think?"

I laughed and Julie continued.

"Why didn't you answer my email?"

"Umm…" I was about to answer that I had just forgotten to turn on the computer in all the bustle of things, but how would that sound?

Julie saved me from having to answer. "Do you want me to come to Wyoming or not?"

"Of course! You know I do!"

"When?"

"As soon as possible! Really, Julie, I thought that was common knowledge."

"Then I'll come day after Christmas," she promised. "I'm already ready to find a little more space than I can find anywhere around here. I'm afraid I'm developing a case of holiday claustrophobia."

"I'm not sure I can promise you much space here," I warned, glancing around the crowded room, then rethought it, "except, of course, for the endless miles of the Wyoming plains and mountains and canyons and valleys filled with nothing but trees and antelope and snow."

"I have a feeling I won't mind the close quarters once I arrive," Julie said seductively, and I thought about Andrea listening in again.

I asked about her family and the beach and we talked for a long time before we hit our first moment of silence.

"So when do I pick you up?" I asked, moving the conversation along.

"I'll change my reservations right now and email you the

itinerary. It'll probably cost an arm and a leg to make a change so close to Christmas."

"I'll make it worth your while," I promised. I remembered the small felt-lined box in my duffel bag upstairs and its sparkling surprise inside. It looked like I would have the chance to give her the perfect gift this Christmas after all!

"That will be easy," Julie said. She had no idea what she was in for. "I love you."

"I love you, too," I said. "Can't wait to see you." We said goodbye and already I couldn't wait to start making plans for how I would propose.

But one thing was sure. I would not propose to her in this house. As I hung up the phone, I looked around the living room and found everyone quietly watching me. I hadn't even noticed that even the piano had stopped playing.

"Oooh," Alisha teased in a sing-song voice. "Spencer has a girlfriend!"

Six days. I could hardly wait.

29 Time Stands Still

The next few days passed slowly in my eagerness for Julie to arrive, but one by one, they ended just the same.

At some point, I emerged sufficiently from my own little world to notice that Ski didn't seem as happy as he had been. He sometimes spent hours sitting alone on the back porch, bundled up against the cold, just staring out over the empty fields and watching the steam of his breath rise and vanish in the frigid air. I realized that I had neglected him.

One afternoon, I caught him rummaging through the large back closet.

"Looking for something?" I asked.

"Yeah. Got any size-ten ski boots I can use?"

I pointed to a large wooden footlocker near the back of the closet.

Once he had tried on a pair and seemed satisfied, he picked up a pair of skis and poles and headed for the back door. "See ya in a few hours," he said.

"Wait up," I answered, "I'll show you around the neighborhood."

Ski was a bit wobbly and awkward on his skis At first,, but I

The Perfect Gift

gave him some pointers on how to hold the poles low and use them to push, how to kick a little extra at the end of each step and let his skis slide a few inches before taking his next step, and he soon grew comfortable and steady.

"I wonder if it was worth it," Ski said out of the blue after a few minutes of skiing silently alongside by side.

"What?" I asked.

Ski didn't answer for a few minutes and I waited patiently. "For a few days," he began, "I felt better than I have ever felt in my life."

"And now?"

"Terrible. Miserable. I ache all over inside. But it might have been worth it."

"You make it sound like the two are related, like you feel miserable now *because* you were happy then."

"Don't you think so?" he asked. "I mean, what other explanation is there? Isn't that why everyone hates Mondays? Because they just got used to the weekend, just got a taste of what a life of leisure could be like, and then they're shoved back into reality, back into the drudgery of real life."

I didn't know what to tell him. I knew there was something wrong with his analysis, that permanent happiness was possible, but I didn't know what path would take him from here to there.

"Follow me," I directed, then turned off the snow-packed road we had been skiing along. We cut through fields with occasional dry wheat or corn stalks protruding from the snow. We reached a small canyon cut between sloping foothills and started up a narrow path between the trees. Soon we reached a solid wall of trees and I led Ski through the dense branches to emerge in a magical clearing set between tall, dark pines.

Ski was breathing heavily by the time we stopped in the center of the clearing. I hoped the exertion would help clear his mind the way it always seemed to work for me.

"It's beautiful," he said once he began to catch his breath.

"This is where I spent last New Year's Eve," I told him. "We made a fire and sat here all night long until the sky turned pink."

"You and Annetta?" he asked. I nodded. "It's a long way from Time Square," he observed.

"Kind of reminds you that time is something we sort of invented just so we could measure it and watch it go by, doesn't it?" I mused. "And I wonder, if we weren't always watching the clock, if time would just stop and stand still. That's how I felt here."

"That sounds nice," Ski sighed.

"What does?"

"Time standing still."

"I thought you just said you were feeling miserable. Why would you want time to stand still now?"

Ski flashed me what would have been an annoyed look if he hadn't looked so tired. "If time stood still, I would have all the time in the world to learn everything."

"What's the rush?" I asked. "You can never know *everything*." Even as I argued the point, though, I began to see what he meant. If time had truly stood still one year ago in this tiny clearing, then I would have had enough time to get to know Annetta better. I wouldn't have left her a few days later and she wouldn't have flown off to France a few weeks after that. I wouldn't have spent months angry and disappointed and confused.

But I might not have dated and fallen in love with Julie, either. And Julie wouldn't be coming here in a few more days and I wouldn't be slipping a sparkling diamond onto her finger and living happily ever after. So you see? Everything always works out for the best in the end.

Of course if Annetta really had kept me from Julie, that means things would have worked out with her instead. It means we could have spent all kinds of time together, and that we would possibly be together and married right now.

But Julie is reality, and I couldn't ask for anyone better. I had no need to dwell on the past. It never helps to spend too much time wondering what might have been.

30 Good Grief

We started skiing again and Ski's mood seemed to improve significantly by the time we got home. The physical activity had done him good as I knew it would.

Late afternoon sunlight fell against the house's decorative windows and woodwork as we drew near, with a light so warm you'd have expected to find the air temperature a matching, comfortable, summer-like seventy or eighty degrees. We scraped the snow from our skis and carried them back inside to their closet. Sounds of a movie playing upstairs echoed down the stairwell and explained the relative peace and quiet downstairs.

After changing clothes, we sat on the floor upstairs, leaning against the wall, and watched the movie over the heads of kids lining nearly every spare inch of carpet between us and the television. After a few minutes, Ski stood up and carefully made his way through the small bodies and "Hi, Ski!"s and back downstairs. I didn't think much of it and let him go.

The show ended an hour later and became a double feature with an old holiday favorite popular enough to entice most people to stay. I excused myself and wandered downstairs. The floor wasn't comfortable enough to sit on for two more hours.

I wandered into the kitchen to look for something to snack on, then into the living room where I found Grandma sitting on the couch reading. "Have you seen Ski?" I asked. Grandma glanced up and shook her head. I walked back upstairs to our room to see if he wanted to drive into town just in case we found anything to do there, even though I knew we wouldn't. The room was empty, with our coats and everything just the way we had left them. I walked past the bathroom but found it with the door open and empty. Finally I glanced out the back door, and sure enough, there sat Ski, leaning against the house, staring out across the empty fields, with the cool evening light shining down on his shivering body.

"What's up?" I asked.

I sat down next to him and wished I had brought my coat outside with me.

"I think I need to see a doctor," Ski said after another minute of staring in silence. "I'm not feeling so hot."

"I think you need your coat," I told him. "How long have you been sitting out here?"

Ski glanced at me briefly and ignored my question.

"What's wrong?" I asked.

"I have no idea," Ski answered. "I just have some kind of ache inside, and it keeps getting worse."

I watched him with a concerned look on my face and he continued.

"At first, I thought I was just in a bad mood or just experiencing a little discomfort from changing my comfort zones so much. Now, it's like I want to cry all the time, but it won't come out, and crying would only make it worse."

Ski looked at me with both eyebrows raised slightly in consternation, then said again, "Spence, I think I need to see a doctor. This is kind of freaking me out. Do you think anyone in this town is qualified to help with something like this?"

"Let's go ask Gramma," I answered. She would know what to do. I stood up and held out a hand to pull Ski to his feet. His hand felt cold and his teeth began to chatter as we stepped back inside the house.

We found Grandma still sitting alone in the living room, and once Ski had explained his condition to her, she asked a few questions and offered her diagnosis.

"It's perfectly natural," she assured him. "You're grieving."

Ski considered this prognosis with a slight grimace of pain, then cocked his head to one side and asked "Grieving for what?"

"For everything you're letting go of."

"Like what?"

"Like whatever pain you've been carrying around inside and ignoring ever since you were a child. Like whatever beliefs you've been living about the kind of person you are and the kind of life that's available to you. Like your ideas about whether or not you're capable of loving and being loved."

Grandma's words obviously struck a chord, because Ski stood up then, said a quick "Excuse me," and left the room. We heard the back door open and close, and a muffled sob from the back yard.

31 Physical Therapy

When Ski didn't return for over ten minutes, I got his coat from our room and carried it outside. I didn't find him sitting on the porch, but heard the heavy *thwak*s of the ax chopping wood in the barn.

I stepped across the yard and stopped in the open doorway. There stood Ski next to the wood pile, now nearly overflowing with chopped wood. Traces of half-dry tears streamed down his face and stopped at the corners of his mouth which now smiled broadly, though his eyes still sparkled with half-tears.

He stopped swinging the ax, letting the head rest on the ground and leaning on its shaft. Ski then did perhaps the only thing he had ever done to surprise me. He laughed. Twice. The real thing, too, from all the way deep down in his stomach. He seemed to enjoy it so much that he did it once more, and then spoke. "I don't know what your grandmother did," he said, "but...."

He didn't have the words to explain, so he just raised his

palms in the air as if to say *Look at me!* "It's like all that misery is just letting go, and I have never in my entire life felt this bad and this good all at the same time!" Ski laughed once more, which instantly sent tears leaping from his eyes again. "I feel great!" he announced simply.

32 Revolution

Every now and then Ski still felt the ache, but he reported that it now usually came accompanied by a sweetness that made it pleasant and comfortable, or at least bearable. Grandma explained that this was all part of the process of healing. She pointed out that Ski must have been very ready for this change to occur because it all happened so unusually fast.

Ski explained it to me one evening like this: "They never tell the story of the Tin Man after Dorothy left."

"What happens?" I asked.

"Well, he got his heart and sometimes hearts do things like this. Sometimes they hurt. He probably missed Dorothy, you know. I think sometimes having a functional heart is as much of a curse as a blessing."

I awoke with a start early one morning before the sky outside had begun to grow light and realized that a shoe had just landed on my chest. I had been dreaming of slow dancing with Julie.

"Do you realize what this *means*?" Ski asked excitedly when I sat up to see where the shoe came from.

"That you don't want your shoe anymore?" I guessed.

"Just think!" he exclaimed. "This is going to revolutionize my entire life! This changes *everything!* Who'd have guessed?!"

"Congratulations," I said unenthusiastically, then turned over and tried to fall quickly back asleep and resume the dream where I left off.

33 Hopes & Fears

Christmas Eve dinner was simple but good with a ham and half a dozen dishes of vegetables and breads. After getting used to fast food and frozen meals in college, anything homemade always tasted fantastic.

After dinner, everyone gathered in the living room. We didn't have enough furniture to seat everyone, but the kids didn't mind spreading out on the warm carpet near the wood-burning stove.

The traditional program began with a prayer from Saedi. She thanked God for Grandma and everyone else in the family, for Christmas, for Jesus, and for Santa Claus. She prayed for blessings for all of us, and also for the poor and lonely people.

Once she finished and looked around the room to receive the many smiles of love and approval, a few copies of the Bible opened to the second chapter of Luke and we began to read. Each person took a verse. As someone read the part about there being no room in the inn, I saw Diane look over at Ski sitting in one corner of the room and mouth the words "Motel Five." Ski grinned and nodded back.

Dad read the last verse, "And Jesus increased in wisdom and stature, and in favor with God and man." Everyone remained silent for a moment, pondering the chapter, searching for a bit of added meaning on this one special night of the year, and waiting for someone to take charge and move the program along.

"Well?" Dad finally said. "What shall we sing first?"

Kellie was already sitting at the piano bench and spun around toward the keys. "Anything you want," she announced.

"How about *Oh, Little Town of Bethlehem*?" Dad asked, and we all opened our hymn books.

"Dad?" Diane asked once we had finished," why does the song say 'hopes and *fears*'? 'Cause Jesus isn't scary."

"Well," Dad began. "I never really thought about that. But I suppose it's for people who are afraid that maybe they'll get in trouble for not keeping the commandments and for not being kind to others like Jesus taught."

"Oh."

I watched Ski sitting cross-legged on the floor in the corner. A three-year old had scooted into his lap to share his hymn book, and Ski mouthed the words quietly as everyone else sang.

When we finished singing most of the Christmas hymns, I stood up and motioned for Ski to follow me outside. We closed the door behind us and stood still in the bright light of a full moon. It cast heavy shadows on the snow beneath us. I thought of the new star that led the wise men to the Christ child two thousand years ago.

The Perfect Gift

"I know what the fear is that Di asked about," Ski said.

"Oh, yeah?" I asked. "What?"

"It's the fear that it's not real. The fear that it won't really work. Or that it won't last."

I wanted to say *It will! It will!* but I knew that Ski would have to learn this lesson for himself, so I kept quiet.

"I mean," Ski continued, "what happens when we go home? If I crack under pressure, what will I find inside?"

"Whatever you find there," I answered, "will be better than anything that *doesn't* come from inside."

"Hm," Ski responded thoughtfully.

34 Paintings

I awoke Christmas morning at 5:30 a.m. to the shuffle of Diane's slippered feet creeping into my room. I wondered how long she had been awake. The rule said that you couldn't set your alarm and you couldn't wake anyone up before seven. Of course, if someone happened to wake up while you were creeping around the house in slippers, well that was their own problem.

Diane waited at the side of my bed silently, and I opened one eye a crack to see what she was up to. She had been watching me, and now she leaned closer to see if my eyelid had really moved. I thought about jumping up and startling her, but her scream would wake the rest of the house.

"Diane, what are you doing?" I whispered.

"Oh, I was hoping you'd wake up!"

Outside, wind battered the shutters and shingles, sending occasional shivering creaks down through the house's frame or whispers down the wood burning stoves' chimneys. I got up and walked downstairs with Diane's hand in mine. I tossed a few more logs into the stove and sat down on the couch, my arm around Di's shoulder, staring at the Christmas tree lights flashing off and on from floor to ceiling.

Soon a pair of young cousins came walking down the stairs behind us, their eyes still half shut. They walked together to the edge of the tree and presents scattered below it and lay down on the warm carpet. Within seconds, they had fallen asleep again.

I dozed off as well and woke an hour later when everyone began filtering downstairs. Bathroom doors could be heard opening and closing, and Grandma walked into the kitchen to prepare a snack of fruit and cereal for anyone hungry enough to eat.

"What's the matter, Spencer?" Ski asked, sitting down on the couch next to me. "Afraid you wouldn't get a good seat?"

"Huuurrrry!" whispered Saedi, anxiously holding her first gift and waiting for everyone to arrive so she could open it.

Soon everyone had gathered and we began opening one gift at a time—a tradition begun in years when there wasn't enough money for many gifts—to make opening them take longer and make it seem like we had more of them.

Alisha tore slowly at one corner of her gift from me. "It's green...oh, it's a shirt! Thanks Spencer!" She held it up against herself as everyone commented on how well it matched her blonde hair.

"I did that on purpose," I told her.

Alisha stepped around the tree and pulled out the next gift.

This went on for a while, and then a gift came out for me. It was from Grandma. It was a heavy box about eight inches long, six high, and four across. I shook it lightly to make sure I didn't break anything inside.

"I have no idea," I confessed, and began to open it. From inside the box, I pulled a beautiful hardwood sculpture of a stallion rearing up on its hind feet atop a rocky ridge. Its mane blew wildly in the wind. The dark wood showed even darker swirls of grain and created a beautiful illusion of seeing the horse in silhouette through a swirling mist. "Wow, thanks, Gramma! It's beautiful!"

"I thought you'd like that," she answered, smiling. "A local artist carved it."

After Diane opened her next gift, she walked around the tree and found a rolled up sheet of paper, tied with a blue ribbon. This she brought to Ski. He untied the ribbon and unrolled a finger-painting of pine trees, snow, stars, and a few oddly-shaped musical notes with the words 'Merry Christmas' and 'I love you' written above and below them.

"Spencer said you wanted one," she informed him. It was true that Ski had told me he wanted one of my sister's finger paintings that she often sent me in the mail, but he had said so sarcastically. Now he really did appreciate it and thanked Diane with a hug.

Gift giving made a few more rounds, and the anxiousness wore off the children as their small piles of toys grew. I gave Ski a pass to Beaver Mountain, the ski resort up the canyon from school.

"You'll have to teach me," he said.

"Sure thing," I promised. "It's high time you learned to live up to your name."

Alisha got a cordless phone from Mom and Dad. "This isn't a cell phone," she complained.

"We've already discussed that," Dad said. "You'll be old enough for a cell phone in a few years."

Alisha pouted momentarily, then said, "I love you anyway," and hugged them both.

I got an electronic picture frame, two shirts, a ski pass, and a few books and other trinkets. Then came Ski's third gift.

Ski carefully tore back the paper from a beautifully framed water color painting of the canyon above Amber, at the edge of the Wind River Mountains in springtime. This gift came from Grandma. She spent some of the warmer months hiking with her easel and paint set, dipping her brush in crystal, bubbling streams as she spread the paint across the paper.

I had a pair of her paintings hanging in my room at school, and each had a quote that Grandma carefully selected.

In the lower right corner of Ski's painting she had painted the words "In the ongoing masterpiece of mortality, every brushstroke we apply, each drop of paint that falls, every action we take and fleeting thought that spills through our minds, fills the canvas of our lives and sometimes covers over the past."

"Thanks a lot!" Ski said gratefully.

After a late breakfast and shower, I found Ski downstairs finishing up the dishes. Grandma scolded him. "You didn't have to do these!"

"Actually, I did," Ski returned. "It's in my contract—you have to read the fine print, though."

Grandma wrapped one arm around Ski's waist and gave him a hug. Ski hugged her back and I noticed how comfortable he looked.

Later on, out in the barn, Ski picked up the ax again and began chopping more wood.

"Hey, Spencer," he shouted when I stepped out onto the porch, "check me out! I'm doin' the dude ranch thing! Most people have to pay hundreds of dollars to do this in the heat of Arizona summers. Not me though, no siree! I'm livin' the high life for free!"

35 Good News

Julie called in the afternoon and I was glad that Alisha had plugged in and charged her new cordless phone so I could take the call in the relative privacy of my room.

"Do you want the good news or the bad news?" She asked.

"Just the good," I requested. "Why don't you save any bad news for when I pick you up tomorrow? Unless it's just that you miss me."

"I *do* miss you," Julie admitted. "But..." I got the feeling I was about to get the bad news. "My dad was fixing the Christmas lights on the roof last night, and he fell off."

For a moment I feared the worst.

"He's okay," she quickly reassured me, "but he broke his leg and a few ribs and is feeling pretty miserable today." I breathed a sigh of relief. "Would it be okay..." she paused, then continued, "if I come down a day or two later? It would mean a lot to him if I stuck around."

"Of course," I answered. I felt disappointed and would miss her a little extra since I had planned to see her so soon, but that would be okay. "What's the good news?"

"I love you," she whispered.

I felt better then. "I love you, too," I whispered back.

Julie went on to tell me about hiking her favorite trail that led to a swing hanging from a giant tree at the crest of a hill, about the beautiful dunes along the beach, and how she had forgotten how much she loves the ocean. "But I couldn't stop wishing you could have been there, too, so I could show it all to you."

She wished I could meet and get to know her family, that I could be there with my arm around her while they watched movies, and be on her team for board games. "We'd never lose," she declared.

We discussed me driving out to Oregon instead of her flying back early, but I told her about Ski and his transformation and we both agreed that we should try not to interrupt it.

After we hung up, I reached into my duffel bag and pulled out a small package wrapped in metallic green paper that I had planned to save until tomorrow when she arrived. I held it in my hands for a moment, deciding. Then very slowly, I tore away at the corners of the shiny wrapping paper. It would help me wait, I decided, it would help me be patient.

Inside the paper, I found a silver picture frame. In the glass

The Perfect Gift

were etched our names, *Spencer & Julie*. Behind the glass was my favorite picture of us, one taken of Julie and I late last summer at the dam, the sun shimmering on the water behind us, a distant water skier kicking up a tall, back-lit rooster tail of spray, our tan skin showing a hint of sunburn, our white teeth and eyes flashing, my toned arms wrapped around her slender waist and Julie leaning back against my chest and laughing.

On the back of the frame, she had written in permanent marker:

No matter what happens between us, Spencer,
the time we have spent together means more to me
than anything I have ever known.
No matter what happens,
your love and friendship and thoughtfulness
have left deep and permanent etchings on my life.
No matter what happens,
I will love you forever.
Julie

For long minutes, I did nothing but turn the frame from front to back, first staring at our faces in the picture, then reading and rereading the words. *A perfect gift*, I thought, and was glad I had chosen to open it now.

I finally reached into my duffel bag again and pulled out another box, this one small and red. I flipped it open and stared at the diamond, then held it up next to the Julie's picture.

"Two or three days," I thought out loud. "That's a long time."

36 Bad News

Julie called again that night. I carried the cordless phone up to my room again and again Julie asked, "Do you want the good news or the bad news?"

"Do I really get a choice this time?" I asked.

"All the flights are full," she announced. "The only one left before New Year's Eve isn't until the 30th, is first class, and with the change fee at such late notice, would cost me over a thousand dollars."

"What's the good news?" I asked, my face curling up into a disappointed grimace.

"I was kind of hoping you could help me with that this time," Julie said, sounding defeated. "I'm having a hard time thinking of any."

I told her I had opened her gift and absolutely loved it. She asked if I had found her the perfect gift yet. "You're going to love it," I promised.

We spoke for a little while longer, then hung up, reassuring each other that once the next eight days had passed, they would be over and forgotten.

It was better, I thought, to have expected her to come. At least it gave me something to look forward to for a while, something to hope for, something always just a few days out in the future, something to keep me holding on.

37 Magic

A day or two later, I found myself alone in my room, laying on the bed, staring at Julie's picture. All I could think about was that she ought to have been here by now. I wasn't doing a very good job of being patient, nor of appreciating the holidays and all the opportunities to enjoy my family that I would regret not taking advantage of once vacation had passed.

I tried to think of something that might take my mind off Julie for a while, but in comparison to even thinking about her, nothing sounded very fun. I glanced around the room for something else to do and the shoe box with Netta's letters caught my eye, sitting atop the roll top desk where I left it.

I found the envelopes with the pictures and dumped them out, then held one up next to Julie to compare. Because I had no pictures of Netta of my own, I had never been able to compare the two girls side by side. I noticed their different features, each beautiful in her own way. Julie looked like a model, while Annetta had great features and her own unique charm.

The next thing I noticed was how differently each girl made me feel. Looking at Julie made me aware of the excitement and anticipation of days to come. She made me feel loved and lucky that such an incredible girl would fall in love with me.

Staring at Annetta's picture momentarily brought back a tinge of the old disappointment, but that quickly faded away.

I sat down on the edge of my bed with the photos and began to remember what came before the disappointment. I stared at Annetta's eyes and saw in them her love of the world and her ability to capture all its beauty with a single glance. *What an amazing person she is*, I admitted to myself. Another feeling also returned to memory, but I couldn't quite define it.

Whatever it was, though, brought back the impression that life is chock full of magic. That every moment is a miracle. Every morning filled to overflowing with wonder. I hadn't felt this way for a long time, not since Netta and I were still close. I had forgotten all about it.

That must have been what I loved most about her, I thought, though I hadn't been so aware of it back then.

And suddenly I knew how to keep myself busy and keep time passing by quickly. Suddenly I had a worthwhile goal. I would learn how to see the world this way on my own. I felt sure that if I held onto this feeling long enough, if I could watch the world go by and look for pockets of magic in any given moment, then I would no longer need Annetta to remind me how.

I stared into her green eyes for a few minutes longer to get a solid hold on this feeling, then tossed the pictures into the box and headed downstairs.

38 Perspective

I went downstairs and played games with the children. I helped cook and wash dishes. I went for a run down the road. I sat at the third-story window and watched the sun sink its red fire over the white Wind River Mountains and sat in my room listening to the wind buffet the house in the darkness. And while I found pockets of beauty here and there, the main thing I learned was that developing this outlook on the world was harder than I expected. I had to keep glancing at Annetta's eyes to remind myself what I was looking for.

But the beginning of any trek into unfamiliar territory is always the difficult part. I awoke the next morning still determined to learn. Surely it would get easier with time and experience.

Within the hour, I found the perfect opportunity. Kellie had invited Jim over for breakfast, and as he carried his dishes to the kitchen after breakfast, he mentioned that Mr. McCourt's cows had broken a fence and wandered off into the foothills. Jim had been hired to help round them up.

"Need any help?" I asked.

"Know how to ride a horse?" Jim asked in return, and forty five minutes later found me sitting in a saddle, my feet in the stirrups, trotting out of Mr. McCourt's barnyard on a beautiful beige mare.

"This is great fun, Jim," I said with a silly grin spread all the way across my face. "Thanks for bringing me along!"

Jim just nodded in response and chewed on a thought for a while before commenting. "Some things in life are worth more than others. Once you figure out what they are, you'd best get as much of those things as you can manage."

We rode along the roadside for a while, then turned along the fence line to the break where the cows had escaped. From there, we followed a winding trail up a dry creek bed and shallow ravine leading into the foothills. The snow was shallow and showed the cattle's path easily.

I thought about my goal again and determined to ask Jim about it in case he had any insight into my quest. In his fashion, I spent the next few minutes formulating my question. When the ravine reached the top of the first rise, the trail widened and I prodded my horse up next to Jim's.

"Does the world ever look magic to you, Jim?"

Jim took his standard pause before answering. It was a good thing we had all day for this conversation. "It's funny," he began, "seems like when everything's going good and comfortable, well, that's nice. But when things get rough, that's when the real beauty kicks in. Like when it's twenty below and blowing. Or when a calf is being born breach. Then you don't have time to just stroll along. Then the only thing that matters is what you do *right now*. And then suddenly you're wide awake and you notice how beautiful it all is."

Those were the most words I had ever heard Jim utter at one time. And I was glad I had asked, they gave me a few clues for where to look to find the magic. The ravine grew narrow again and I dropped back behind Jim to think everything over.

When the ravine widened and I got a chance to ride up next to him again, I asked "Do you think it's possible to learn to see things that way *all* the time?"

Jim pursed his lips to think and then shook his head.

The Perfect Gift

"Sounds like it might take an awful lot of effort. Besides, those moments might not be as special if you felt that way all the time."

He had a good point, but I still didn't give up on the goal. Even if life didn't *always* feel magic, I at least wanted to feel that way more often.

"Seems like some people never recognize any beauty," I commented, "and others see it all the time. Like maybe they're *part* of the beauty, like they're caught up in the river of it and it comes pouring out of their eyes."

"Ah," Jim simply answered, nodding knowingly. "I see what you're getting at. I remember that, too."

I felt glad to know that someone else understood. "I just want to get as much of it as I possibly can, that's all," I explained.

"That's the right idea," he agreed.

The ravine opened up to a wide meadow, full of shallow snow with tall grasses poking through. Here the cattle tracks spread out in every direction and two dozen head could be seen scattered over half a mile in either direction. The sun came out from behind the high, thin clouds, and everything shone brilliant white.

My horse wanted to run, I could tell, and no wonder, it was such a perfectly beautiful place. Straining at the bit, I held her back and waited for my instructions. I nodded my head slightly toward the mare. "She sure seems to recognize beauty, doesn't she?"

Jim nodded in agreement. "Like nobody else I've ever met."

It sounded strange for Jim to compare a horse to people, or did he refer to horses *as* people? My horse's muscles tightened, ready to leap forward the moment I let the reins go slack. "She's so alive," I said, feeling excited to see what would happen once I let her go. "I can feel it just being near her."

Jim smiled at my enthusiasm and nodded again in agreement.

"Seems like if I just let her go," I continued, "she'd never stop running and never look back."

Now it was Jim's turn to shoot me a quizzical look, though I didn't know why.

"What now?" I asked, eager to be off and galloping through the snow. "Do I start the chase?"

Jim gave me another funny look. "Are we talking about Netta?" he asked.

39 Alive

When I explained that I was referring to my horse, Jim laughed out loud. "Yeah," he said with an amused glint in his eye, "let 'er go. She knows what to do. We'll meet back here."

Jim said he would search the canyons and ravines above for other strays, and I let my horse go as Jim trotted away.

She first ran to the south end of the meadow, kicking up snow and mud behind us the entire way. I held on tightly to her mane and the saddle horn, clenched my teeth, and prayed that I wouldn't fall off.

Once we had passed up all the cattle, the horse wheeled and trotted toward the cows. As we neared the first heifer, it looked up nervously with its big, brown eyes but didn't budge. For a moment the horse hesitated as if confused. "Haa!" I shouted instinctively, and the cow turned and began trotting away. "Haaaaa!" I yelled again, feeling silly but thoroughly enjoy myself.

I patted my mare appreciatively on the neck and wished I knew her name instead of just saying "Good horsey." Before I knew it, we had the entire south end of the meadow rounded up into a group near the trail, and the horse took off again at a gallop to clean up the other end. I had never felt quite so alive.

Out of the corner of my eye, I watched as Jim guided a few strays into the meadow. He watched me for a moment and nodded his approval, then headed up another draw to continue his search.

When my horse and I finished our task, Jim was nowhere to be seen. We stopped near the herd that had begun to fan out again as the cows wandered aimlessly and chomped at anything protruding from the snow.

While I worked, I had no time for anything but enjoying the moment. Now I let my thoughts travel back to my goal of learning to see the world from Annetta's point of view.

But the moment I turned my thoughts in that direction, I realized that I no longer needed to try. I felt awake and happy. I could hardly understand why I ever worried about seeing beauty in the first place. I had always loved the outdoors and always soaked in its beauty and let it affect me for days afterward, adding a happy, content note to my mood which only slowly faded away. All I needed was to get outside and get moving and let nature do its job.

I swung one leg over the horse and stepped down to the ground to walk and kick through the snow until Jim returned. Besides, my rear end was getting sore, though just as Jim had

The Perfect Gift

pointed out, even that sensation added to the composite sensation of joy and feeling fully alive.

40 Too Good

Jim dropped me off at home after three o'clock. I grabbed a quick bite of lunch leftovers and headed upstairs for a shower. I noticed how the flavor of the honey mustard and venison on crunchy dinner rolls tasted all the more enjoyable after a good workout. I felt pleased to learn that the optimistic feelings gained from the ride barely abated as time passed. I couldn't have enjoyed the day any more fully.

In my room after a warm shower, I dressed and started thinking about what I would do with the rest of the afternoon and evening, then sat down on my bed and leaned back against the wall. While I thought, I absent mindedly picked up Netta's and Julie's pictures that I had been comparing that morning.

Julie looked even better than she had before, which I attributed to my clearer, happier mood. Feeling good makes everything look better.

Then I glanced at Netta's photo, and my mood took a noticeable dip. My happy smile dimmed.

It wasn't that she didn't look great. It wasn't that she didn't make me feel good. It was that she made me feel *too* good, and I realized that the great mood I had worked myself into came nowhere near to the beauty that shone from her eyes.

It was an entirely different sensation and clearly unique to her. I had failed to learn it after all.

41 Under Pressure

Warm sunlight spilled all over the bedspread from the window when I woke up Saturday morning. Ski had already left the room and I lay there alone for a few more minutes. Outside the door, sounds of people running up and down the stairs echoed through the hall. As I got up and headed for the shower, I heard the call to come to breakfast, and then that we should hurry so we could get out snowmobiling sooner.

There was still plenty of food when I made it down to the dining room, and I finished eating just as everyone else finished loading the sleds on the trailer. "Perfect timing," I thought to myself.

We drove into the mountains and began unloading the snowmobiles. It quickly became apparent that there were too many helping hands, so as soon as we pulled the first machine off the trailer, I started it up and called to Ski.

"Hey! Hop on the back and I'll show you how this is done. All ya gotta do is squeeze the throttle here." Without another word, I opened the throttle all the way and the sled jumped into action. Ski threw his arms around my waist to keep from being thrown off the back as we charged toward the canyon. Without even looking, I sensed the rooster tail of snow spitting out behind us as we sped along a narrow ridgetop.

The rush of power and speed brought back instant reminders of yesterday's heightened awareness of beauty and adventure and feeling truly alive.

I squeezed the throttle harder in hopes of driving those feelings deeper into my heart and mind. It worked. The snowmobile under our bodies skipped across the slightly uneven powder trail. Ski held on tighter and I knew he felt scared because I found it hard to draw in a full breath of air.

Twenty feet to either side of our ridge, the snow fell away, sometimes slowly, sometimes quickly, to a pair of ravines which then rose again to other pine-covered slopes.

A hundred yards ahead, the abrupt end of our ridge came into sight, with the same cliff Annetta had driven me over last year. I pressed the throttle harder, and the machine picked up speed—now zooming over the snow's surface at over forty miles per hour.

As the brink approached, I felt Ski squeeze harder till I could hardly breathe. "He's trying not to show his fear," I thought, "but I'm reading it loud and clear." Finally he broke down.

"Spencer—the cliff! Can this thing stop?"

But it was too late. Just then, we reached the edge of the cliff and the snow dropped abruptly away below us. Wind screamed through our ears as the engine suddenly went quiet and we fell and fell through the cold air.

Ten feet after we left the top of the cliff, the steep powder caught us gently. The sled landed perfectly, with the skis just higher than the rear of the machine. We landed just before the ground began to rise again and the steepness made the transition between dropping and landing more gradual. The whole thing felt like slow motion.

"You are insane! Let me off this thing before you kill us!"

"As you wish."

We headed back up the ravine and returned to the parking lot. Everyone else had just finished taking the snowmobiles off the trailer. Diane's smile looked as happy to see me as Ski's expression of mingled fear and relief to get off. She ran over to give me a bear hug, padded by her thick parka. "I getta ride with you, okay, Spencer?"

"Okey dokey!" Now I went to the truck and pulled out a pair of helmets. "Hey, Ski, you'll wanna wear this."

"Oh, yeah, now that the safe stuff is outta the way, I guess I'd better!" He sounded angry, but I knew it wouldn't last.

"Alisha, you go with Ski, okay?" Diane said, with a tone of finality that made it sound more like a command than a question.

Ski looked over at Alisha to see how she felt about the set up. Alisha smiled back and asked, "Have you driven one of these before?"

"Oh, yeah," Ski replied. "We used to drive 'em to school when I lived in Michigan." I doubted if Ski had ever even been to Michigan.

Soon everyone had their helmets on and began making their way slowly down the ravine. Ski pulled on his helmet and gave the starter cord a few quick tugs.

"You might want to open the choke," Alisha said, and pulled up on a small black lever.

Ski gave her a sort of irritated look and said, "Oh, yeah. Our machines in Michigan had automatic chokes." He tugged on the starter once more and the engine roared to life. They climbed on, and started off with a jerk. The four of us then followed the others down the ravine which was quickly becoming a packed trail.

"Yahoo! It feels good to be riding one of these again!" Ski began to experiment. He opened the throttle a little wider and shot off the track and up along the steep side of the ravine. Before the hill stole his speed, he looped around and came zooming back down the hill. "Not bad," I thought out loud.

After a few turns and loops in the powder, Ski pulled back up alongside us and threw me a nervous look. I was surprised—he had looked so comfortable, so confident, so natural. Why did he look nervous now? As it turned out, I didn't want to know.

He glanced at me again, then pressed the throttle all the way down with his thumb and turned, steering up to the ridgetop where I first took him. "He wouldn't dare!" I thought, but the roar of his engine told me otherwise.

We had almost caught up to the slow moving group and I opened my throttle and shot out around them. Everyone waved as I flew by, but I didn't have time to wave back.

It was too late to chase Ski up the ridge and try to stop him. I just raced to the end where I might at least see what happened. "Ski," I whispered, "Don't go as fast as I did! You've never jumped before!"

Both sleds reached the ridge's end at the same time. With one look I could see that Ski was going much faster than I had. I could still see the black tank-like tracks below the snowmobile as he soared over our first landing place. Alisha's feet came off the running boards and hung in the air as the sled plummeted downward, and she clung desperately to Ski. I heard her piercing scream over the roar of the engine.

Finally, they landed hard with an audible *thump*—the ground had flattened out where they landed ten feet past our previous track. Luckily, the snow was deep and soft enough to prevent disaster. Ski pulled to a stop a little further ahead and pulled off his helmet.

"How'd ya like that?" he shouted to me as I pulled up alongside him.

"I didn't, Ski—that's not your machine and that's *not* your sister!" Now it was my turn to be angry. My face turned red and my blood boiled. "You don't even know...." Before I finished my accusation that Ski hardly knew how to drive, I saw Alisha's face. It was white. Her eyes were wide inside her helmet. Even I had never taken her over anything like that. "What were you thinking?!"

As I asked that question, a twinge of guilt twisted my stomach into a gentle knot. Maybe this was partly my fault for doing the same thing to him. I gulped down a few deep breaths of cold mountain air and tried to calm myself down.

Ski turned to Alisha. "You didn't mind, did ya, Ali?"

I watched Alisha search for the kindest words possible while rubbing her right knee that she must have bruised in the landing. "Well, I didn't exactly enjoy it."

I could tell that her response hurt Ski—he had scared himself, too. He wasn't accustomed to fear, and it must have made him feel vulnerable. Now it made him touchy. "Ah, you're all a bunch o' wimps." He turned to Alisha and his voice turned bitter.

The Perfect Gift

"Next time, say so if you don't want to ride with an expert driver."

Now came Alisha's turn to feel hurt. She had always acted thoughtfully and sweetly, and was entirely unprepared for this outlash. She tried to smile anyway, but quickly had to break eye contact and look away to avoid showing her hurt feelings.

I thought of offering to trade riders, but then I caught Diane's expression. She looked confused. Ski was suddenly acting differently than she had seen before. But the most amazing thing happened when I saw Ski notice the same thing.

He looked almost panicked. His eyes widened a little and his mouth hung slightly opened as he searched for the right words to explain, to justify himself, but such words did not exist. The look of panic increased until he finally turned back to Alisha and blurted, "Hey, Alisha, I was just kidding."

Alisha tried to smile again, but still made no eye contact. Instead, her eyes drifted along far-off ridges. Ski fidgeted a little, then looked back at Diane, and her expression hadn't changed, either. Ski took a deep breath and tried again.

"I'm sorry, Alisha. You're not a wimp. And I'm sorry for not driving more carefully." He looked Alisha full in the eye until she nodded her head once and breathed more easily. Her head rose a little higher and she no longer avoided Ski's eyes quite so much. We sat for a moment in silence, broken only by the low rumble of the other snowmobiles inching their way down the ravine toward us and the moan of the wind rushing through the tops of the pines.

"That's okay," Alisha finally admitted. "I guess it *was* kinda fun." She laughed once, more out of relief than happiness. "Just don't do it again!" she warned.

Ski looked back at Diane and the relief at seeing her relax and smile again showed as his shoulders dropped and the panic left his eyes. I saw no point in me staying mad, so I took a few more deep breaths to let the rest of my tension drift away with the breeze.

42 Return to the Past

By early afternoon, enough adults had tired of riding that Alisha and Diane got their own snowmobiles to drive. Ski took advantage of riding alone to practice jumping small drifts and bumps, side hilling, and other stunts.

After lunch, I made my way up the canyon where Amy had

gotten stuck in the snow last year and turned off my machine just past the large pine tree. I spun around and sat backwards on the seat to stare up at the cornice at the top of a small ridge.

From the moment I thought about going snowmobiling, I knew I would come here. I wanted to remember the night I came here in the blizzard and found Annetta's sister's machine stuck and half buried next to the ancient pine.

I wanted to see the drift I rammed the snowmobile into to start a snow cave where we could safely wait out the worst of the storm. I wanted to remember how I felt that night when I knew what to do and I did it with no hesitation or second thoughts.

I remembered leading Amy up the hill and into the tiny cavern, pulling her close and waiting for her to warm up until I knew she was safe, then falling asleep with her in my arms.

I remembered leaving the cave after the storm passed and finding a world of wind-blown powder and a full moon sinking low over the horizon. I remembered driving home and falling asleep instantly, then waking up to find Annetta waiting in my room to thank me, to apologize for her distance, and to throw her arms around my neck and kiss me for the first time.

I remembered her warm body and soft lips. I remembered her arms holding me close. I remembered her green eyes as she looked into mine and told me she loved me and the way my heart responded....

"Wait," I said, shaking my head to clear my thoughts. I would go back to school and back to Julie in a few days. It had been good to allow myself to remember Netta while I was here, to be honest with myself about my feelings and to learn from old memories and sort them all out, but this was too much. This wasn't right.

I thought of Julie instead. I remembered the last glance I had of her, leaving her apartment on my last night at school. I remembered her face, her arms, her insistence when she pulled my text books from my lap, her smile, and her lips. I remembered her beautiful blue eyes closing when we kissed and then...her eyes opened and they were green. Annetta's face appeared defiantly in my mind.

What have I done? I asked myself. I could focus and clear my thoughts easily enough, but I was suddenly afraid that I would not be able to clear my heart. I had remembered too well, and I could no longer deny that something about Annetta made her unique and special...and that I loved her.

That doesn't change anything, I reminded myself…but the fact remained that I had begun to wonder about what might have been. I had begun to wonder if Annetta's magic might have made me happier than Julie's apparent perfection.

I reached down and felt the lump inside my coat pocket. I had brought the ring with me today. This is where I'd have chosen to give it to Julie if she had come up from Oregon. How would she feel if she knew I was planning to ask her to marry her while day dreaming about kissing another girl?

I didn't want to complicate my life. I didn't want to rekindle any attachments to lost causes and 'what if's. I didn't want to let a memory stand in the way of present reality, of Julie and I.

I knew what to do. I started the snowmobile with a quick tug on the cord, hit the gas, spun around and rode away from this place as fast as I could go.

43 Truth

Running away worked for a few minutes. With the visor open, cold wind on my face felt like a welcome slap holding me tightly glued to the present moment, keeping last year's memories at bay. But I quickly realized that running away made no sense. I'd have to answer this dilemma sooner or later anyway, so why wait?

I found a good view atop a tall hill where I could see the mountain ridges falling away beautifully into the distance. I hit the kill switch and took a few deep breaths of the clear air. "Now, then," I said to myself, "what's going on?"

I missed Annetta. So what? She was a neat girl and we had a great time together last year, why wouldn't I miss her? And I still wanted closure. To see her once more and put the finishing touch on the whole affair.

Maybe I missed her so much because I really missed Julie. Julie was the safer bet, after all; and the better choice for me. She was trustworthy, committed, and easy going enough that we could work through any issue. Once we got back together, maybe I wouldn't have to worry about any of these questions anymore.

But maybe, I had to admit, it went deeper than that. Maybe I was still in love with Netta and maybe I still wanted her. Neither of these possibilities would pose any real problem as long as I wanted Julie more, but for the first time, I paused to consider it. "No sense running from the truth," I reminded myself. "Either way…it's the truth."

I didn't know how to weigh this decision. Since I couldn't see Annetta and compare the two girls, the only solution seemed to not worry about figuring things out, but let time lead me one way or another. Either way, I couldn't lose. "But what good would it do to choose Annetta," I wondered, "if I can't have her anyway?"

And then it occurred to me that maybe I *could* have her. Jim was right after all, I hadn't tried very hard to get her back. I had sent a few messages, that's all. If I really tried, I could surely get another chance. If I wrote more, called, or even flew across the ocean to visit, we could at least get back on speaking terms. And I had every reason to suspect that we'd get along as well as before.

As I opened my mind to the possibility that things might work out with Annetta for the first time in months, a vision unfolded before my eyes of how my life could turn out. I remembered the beauty that she awoke within me and imagined how it would feel to experience that beauty nonstop.

I hadn't wanted to see it, but there really was a significant difference between the two girls, and depending on how you scored them, Julie wasn't necessarily the best choice.

This little brainstorming session had not turned out as I planned. The obvious best choice was supposed to be Julie.

Maybe I didn't want to know the truth after all. I wanted to keep things simple for once. I was in love with Julie and she was in love with me. Julie was a sure thing. Annetta could offer no guarantees and I didn't want to start over and let go of the best shot at happiness I had ever found.

If I could, I would forget the entire idea. I would back up and live on in the perfect bliss of ignorance. I would marry Julie and live happily ever after and never look back.

But once you find the truth, it is not easily brushed aside, and the truth was that I felt afraid.

44 Doubting Thomas

Ski waved as he looked up and spotted me from the canyon floor. He made his way up, stopped his snowmobile next to me and shut off the engine. I glanced at him briefly, then resumed staring into the distance.

"You miss her?" Ski asked. The question required no answer

and I didn't offer one. "You'll be back together soon," he added to the silence. I still had nothing to say. "You wanna change the subject?" he finally asked and I nodded my head.

"How's your heart?" I asked. "Are you still the tin man?"

"No," Ski answered, then thought for a minute before continuing. "I found my heart, but things change slowly. But there's no rush."

We sat in silence for another minute or two.

"Is that the perfect gift?" he asked. The felt box sat open on my handlebars, the diamond sparkling in the sun's bright rays.

"Yeah," I answered matter-of-factly.

"It won't be long till she's wearing that thing and smiling nonstop and breaking hearts left and right." Ski reached over and picked up the box to examine the ring. "Ya know," he added, setting it back on my handlebars, "she's the one thing you've done right in your life."

I wish I felt as sure. I tried to convince myself that a few days with Julie would straighten everything out again, that I would see clearly once more and know that we belonged together forever. So far it hadn't worked.

"At least it *was* the perfect gift," I began.

Ski's head turned slowly toward me. "What do you mean?"

"I don't know," I continued. "This place just got me thinking about Annetta," I explained, "and I sort of miss her, too."

Ski continued to watch me. "So what's the problem?"

"I don't know if I should be giving this to Julie till I've sorted things out better, that's all."

"Haven't you learned anything from me these past two weeks?" Ski asked incredulously. "You know," he hinted, "follow your heart?"

"But what if it only leads to more heartache?" I asked. "What if my heart wants what isn't good for me? You can want things that aren't good for you, can't you?"

"I only have one thing to teach you," Ski said, suppressing a wicked grin. "Come over here."

I looked at him and knew something was up. He clenched a gloved hand into a fist and I laughed.

"I don't think I need that lesson."

"Oh yeah?" Ski objected. "I think you do. Just listen to yourself, trying to justify yourself and ignoring your intuition. Come on over here and I'll show you something that will help."

Ski had a point, I wasn't doing a very good job of listening to my heart and trusting what it told me. But I wasn't about to let Ski punch me. "Okay, listen, I don't have to make any decisions just yet. I have time. And I'll pay better attention to my heart, I promise."

"You'd better," he warned, "because if not...*pow!*" Ski swung his fist through the air in slow motion, demonstrating what would happen if I didn't keep my promise. "Honestly, Spence, how can you even doubt? She's the one right thing you've done in your life."

I looked over at Ski and raised an eyebrow. He hadn't caught on.

"What?" Ski asked after a moment.

"Um...."

"*What?!*" he asked impatiently.

"If I follow my heart right now," I began, "then I'm not sure Julie and I are going to work out."

"What are you talking about?!" Ski nearly shouted at me. "Don't be a fool! She's the best thing that ever happened to you!"

I was startled by Ski's reaction. "That's the thing," I replied. "I'm not sure she's the best thing that ever happened to me."

"How can you think that for a *second?!* You're kidding, right?" Ski asked.

I shook my head slowly.

"Are you telling me that other girl was better than Julie? I'm sorry, Spencer, but I find that hard to believe."

"How would you know? You never even met her."

"If she was so great, why didn't you talk about her more after you got home last year?"

"That was partly your fault," I argued. "You were so intent on getting me together with Julie, there wasn't much room for talking about anyone else."

"That's true," he admitted.

Then I remembered Ski's confession to me in the hot springs. Ski loved Julie, too. I wondered if I had made a mistake by telling him my doubts. But how could I doubt him? How could I suspect that he might become my competition? Not after the loyalty he had just shown me in the way he had encouraged me to go ahead and marry her.

Besides, I could hardly imagine Julie and Ski together. Even with his new heart, he would never become as sensitive as me, and that's what Julie said she liked best about me. Competition was the least of my worries. My only real concern was figuring out what to do with these new possibilities.

"The worst thing about the truth," I mused, "is that it's the truth."

"What do you mean?" asked Ski.

"I mean," I began, "that you can't ignore it, and if you do, it's still there and it's still the truth."

"I see your point. I've spent the better part of my life rejecting the truth about people and the world because it didn't fit in with my preconceived notions. I thought I was so clever but how clever is it to defend your mistakes and expect the world to change so you don't have to? I should have said 'the *worst* part of my life,' because that's a miserable way to live."

I felt like the truth was backing me farther and farther into a corner. Every argument seemed to argue for me to take the more difficult road of giving Annetta another chance. But then I saw another truth. "Ya know what?" I said, "Maybe True Love isn't everything it's cracked up to be."

"Sounds like you're trying to side-step Truth again," Ski observed. He raised his fist and smiled a mock threat.

"No really," I said, holding up one hand to stop him, "if *you* had to choose between True Love and a love who would be true to you, which would you choose?"

Ski nodded his head. "I see your point. So it's a choice between True Love and a *true* love."

"That's what this all comes down to," I summarized, "along with the fact that I don't know anything and all this talk about Annetta is pure guess work."

"Oh," said Ski, cocking his head to one side. "I'm sorry. I thought you promised me you'd listen to your heart."

I looked at Ski, then looked away and didn't answer. Even my little question didn't change the fact that my heart was trying to tell me something that I did not want to hear. *The worst thing about the truth*, I thought again, *is that it's the truth.*

45 The Winding Path

Ski must have said something to Grandma, because she stopped me as I left the kitchen the next afternoon.

"Spencer," she asked, gazing out the window. "Which way is Oakley?" Oakley was a small town nestled in a high mountain valley surrounded by beautiful granite cirques that spent two months every year accessible only by snowmobile. Grandma must have known exactly where it was but I obediently pointed west anyway.

"And if you were going to drive there, which way would you go?"

I pointed south, where the highway led to the narrow road that wound upward into the mountains.

"And you wouldn't mind going south even though you really wanted to go west?"

I shook my head. What was she getting at?

Grandma turned away from the window and placed one hand on my shoulder.

"Sometimes the best route to get where you're going isn't the direct route," she told me. "Even when you can't see far down the road, there is always purpose in messages of the heart."

46 Heart of Flesh

Julie phoned again and we spent a few minutes talking, sharing little stories about things that had happened over the past few days and trying to ignore the slight discomfort that appeared in the occasional silences.

"I can't wait to get home and see you again," I said honestly. That would be easier. Everything would clear up then. "And just wait till you meet Ski!"

"What do you mean 'meet'?" Julie asked. "Did he shave his head or something?"

"He's a completely different person," I explained, though I had a difficult time explaining his transformation in detail. "Hang on," I said, "I'll show you." I found Ski downstairs reading on the couch. "It's for you," I said, handing him the phone.

Ski closed his book and raised the phone hesitantly to his ear. "Hello?" he said into the receiver. He listened for a moment before a grin spread across his face. "I'd love to meet," he said, "Spencer has told me so much about you."

I wandered away to let them talk and didn't see him again until he stepped into the dining room over an hour later. He sat down at the table and watched us play a board game, and declined to play when invited with a quiet "No, thanks." He seemed lost in thought and I chose not to interrupt.

Who knows how long after falling asleep that night, I awoke to the sound of Ski tossing and turning in his bed across the room. I lie awake and wondered what could be keeping him up, then I heard a whispered "Spence, you up?"

"Yeah," I answered. I waited for him to speak again and he finally whispered the question that must have been keeping him awake.

"Do you think people ever change?"

Tricky question. On one hand, of course people change. They learn and grow, develop talents and opinions, mature and progress from stage to stage throughout the entire course of their lives.

On the other hand, maybe they don't. Maybe whatever's deep down in their core never changes. Maybe what appears to be growing up and changing is just working one's way toward that most intrinsic part of a person.

The past few weeks had brought major upheaval to Ski's life. It must have felt confusing and disorienting. He must have wondered if he really knew himself anymore, and his conversation with Julie must have brought his old self and new self into sudden, sharp contrast. Perhaps he just hoped for some reassurance that he was still himself and would not feel lost forever.

"No," I answered, "I don't think people really change. In small ways, of course they do, but deep down, they stay the same person."

"You mean in their heart?" he asked. "That doesn't change?"

"It would take some kind of miracle," I assured him.

Ski tossed and turned for a while longer, then got up and left the room. I heard his feet pad downstairs. I closed my eyes and waited for sleep to come, but now I felt too awake. Fifteen minutes later, I gave up and wandered downstairs. Maybe Ski and I could talk about things. Maybe I would just have a glass of eggnog and go back to sleep.

When I reached the bottom of the stairs, I heard sniffing sounds coming from the living room. I hesitated for a moment, wondering if I should go in, then tip toed into the room and found ski sitting on the couch with a lamp turned on at his shoulder and tears streaming down his face.

I was shocked. I didn't know what to do! I hadn't seen him like this since before Christmas. I thought the worst of the grieving had passed. Two weeks ago, I wouldn't have believed that he was even capable of crying.

Things had seemed to be going so well, what could have suddenly gone so wrong? I felt scared for him. And scared for myself because I felt helpless. I didn't know what to say or do. If things had gotten so bad, how could I possibly make them any better?

But I couldn't turn and walk away now. Not even if he hadn't looked up and seen me, I couldn't just leave without knowing that he would be all right.

"You okay?" I asked. The words sounded squished as if all the pressure I felt inside was pressing down on my jaw, making it hard to open and let the words slip out.

"Listen to this," Ski said between sniffs. "I just opened it and this is the first thing I read."

I looked at Ski's lap and saw the large Bible laying open to some chapter in the Old Testament. Ski sniffed loudly again and read, "A new heart also will I give you, and a new spirit will I put within you: and I will take away the stony heart out of your flesh, and I will give you an heart of flesh."

Ski looked back up at me and another large tear slid down his cheek and fell from his chin. "Is this true?" he asked, almost demanded.

I looked back at him. I looked him in the eye now. "Yes," I said adamantly. I hardly began to understand or appreciate what that verse meant to Ski, but I knew that much. I knew that whatever that book *said* could happen certainly *could* happen.

Ski nodded his head slowly and closed his eyes, sending more hot tears streaming down his face to his jaw and the corners of his mouth. I stood and watched as his entire body shook with silent sobs. I wanted to turn away, to let Ski be alone in this moment, but I couldn't go. And Ski didn't seem to mind.

As the sobs continued, Ski began to smile. The widest smile I had ever seen him give. Little by little, the sobs faded away, or rather, they changed. They almost became laughter. Not Ski's usual laughter from the throat, but something quiet, calm and complete, bubbling up slowly from some new place deep within.

Soon Ski only breathed deeply, then opened his eyes again and stared at the Christmas tree. He looked up at me and I was startled to see an intense, bright light shining out from his steady gaze. Not a physical light, but a near-tangible current of power. Of clarity, hope, and peace.

Finally Ski took one deep breath, closed the Bible and stood up. He walked past me, stopping just long enough to put his hand on my shoulder, tap twice, then squeeze it firmly. He looked me steadily in the eyes for a moment and smiled.

"Imagine that, Geppetto," he whispered hoarsely. "Me – a real boy!"

The Perfect Gift

47 Real

Ski's recovery took a giant leap forward that night and left him permanently changed. He laughed more often, spoke more freely with everyone, and gave frequent hugs to the kids who gratefully accepted the attention and affection. The bright glow in his eyes remained.

The next day grew warm and we headed outside to take advantage of spring-like temperatures and the good mood it spread through the yard. Ski thought of a project and directed us to roll the biggest snowballs possible. When they grew to four feet tall—almost too large to roll—we brought them together and piled one on top of the other. Placing the last two-foot diameter ball on top of the others required a stepladder from the garage.

"Everybody ready?" Ski asked, taking his position atop the ladder.

"Ready!" we shouted.

"Okay, then; one, two, three, lift!" We pushed and lifted the snow ball as high as we could, to where Ski pushed it the rest of the way up and held it in place while the rest of us jumped up to pack snow around the bottom edges. Towering nearly ten feet tall, it was the biggest snowman I had ever seen.

"Hey, what was that Santa-face thing I saw in the barn?" Ski asked.

"Oh, I know!" shouted Diane. She ran to the barn and soon returned carrying an eighteen-inch painted plastic face of Santa Claus. It had once belonged to a lampshade attached to an outdoor lamp, but the back half had broken years ago. Now we pushed the face against the top snowball in our pile, and Santa came to life.

I started packing snow onto Santa's torso to form arms, and others ran into the house for a garbage bag that we could cut up to make buttons and a belt. Someone found an orange bag that we stuffed with crumpled-up newspaper, then attached to Santa's shoulder as he must carry his real bag of toys.

"Toys and coal," Ski reminded us with a wink.

Before Santa reached perfection, others set to work building his sleigh, complete with nine reindeer kneeling in the snow. We brought real deer antlers from the barn and attached them to the reindeer heads, and the front deer got a red Christmas tree bulb for a nose. Thirty feet of baling twine laced around the reindeer's necks for reigns completed the sculpture.

"See, Alisha?" said Diane. "I told you Santa's real." Alisha just shook her head and rolled her eyes.

Di sat in the sleigh and picked up the reins. "Giddy up!" she shouted. "Up, up and away!"

"Diane," said Alisha, "you're supposed to say 'On Dancer, on Prancer, on Comet and Vixen.'"

"Actually," interrupted Ski, "what Santa really said was, 'I'll follow you guys!'"

A day or two later, we noticed more traffic than normal on our usually deserted street. Cars would drive out from town and pass slowly by the house before turning around and heading back to town. Others climbed out of their cars to take a photo with our masterpiece.

48 Stay Forever

The final days of vacation passed by quickly with more games, reading, and talking with the family. We attended church on Sunday and I noticed Ski listening to the talks, deciding what to make of them.

Once or twice I wandered into the living room and caught Ski reading the Bible. He occasionally asked me questions that gave me the impression he was trying to decide if miracles had really caused his changes and whether or not they would last.

"So what you're saying," he said out of the blue one day, "is that the hard part is already over."

I glanced over his shoulder and saw that he was reading toward the end of the Book of John, just after the crucifixion and resurrection. "It's in the bank," I assured him.

"Nailed," he thought out loud. "Sealed up. Sure and secure."

"The good guys won," I affirmed. "The only thing left is to choose which team to join."

The front yard filled up with snow figures of all kinds. Kids had to import snow for the last sculptures by dragging sled-fulls of the white stuff from the fields behind a snowmobile.

Standing just outside the front window stood a five-foot-tall King Kong. Baby New Year and Old Man Old Year sat at a small table playing with real cards. Baby New Year held a royal flush, while the old man had only a pair of deuces. The checker pieces stacked up on the table suggested that Baby New Year would clean up on this hand. Leaning against the fence near the road, a disturbingly-realistic snow baby, made from real children's clothes stuffed with snow, stood and waved at passing traffic.

Ski stood outside directing a so-far unsuccessful attempt to build a reindeer chorus line that wouldn't collapse. New Year's Eve had arrived, and vacation would end for Ski and me tomorrow. Classes would begin in a few days, and we both wanted to beat the long lines by buying books early, before most students returned to campus.

"You've done a great job with the yard, Ski," I said as he stood back from the reindeer and pondered how to make it work. Little cousins gathered around trying to help, beginning their ideas with "I know! Maybe we could..." and ending them with, "Nah, that won't work, either."

"Yeah, but I can't quit wondering what's going to happen when we leave," Ski mused.

"Oh, I doubt anyone around here would knock them down."

"That's not what I'm talking about. I mean what if it doesn't last?"

I looked at Ski. Of course they'll melt, I thought. You knew that would happen when you built them, and there's nothing you can do about it.

Ski glanced up at me, clearly annoyed that I hadn't caught on to what he really meant. "I'm talking about everything, Spence. The whole thing. I mean, this place is different; I'm different here. But what will happen when we go back to school?"

He looked around at the snow sculptures, his eyes squinting in the bright sunshine. "I just don't know what will happen, that's all."

I stopped for a moment and thought. "Remember that painting Gramma gave you? What did the words say?" I asked.

"Something like 'every new thought and action can change our lives and paint over whoever we used to be'."

"Yeah, that's it," I said, nodding. "You've changed, Ski, because of your experiences here. Things back at school may not seem as simple as they are here, but you're different now, and you can never go back to being who you were before."

This seemed to comfort Ski somewhat. "Yeah." He nodded his head slowly. "Thanks."

"And I've got another idea," I said, running inside. "Hang on a sec." A minute later, I emerged with a camera. "Hey, Saedi, wanna take a picture of me n' Ski?"

The four-year-old ran over, anxious to hold what had always been a no-touch item for her.

"I wanna take a picture," chimed three other young voices as I showed Saedi which button to press.

"Some other time, kids," Ski told them. "Saedi's been pneumatically selected for today's random ergonomic chore."

The kids stared blankly at Ski, waiting for their brains to make sense of what he had just said. "Oh," one said. Ski and I sat down in Santa's sleigh with our hands on the reins while Saedi snapped a photo.

"Take one more," I told Saedi, hoping at least one shot would be lined up well in the viewfinder.

"Say cheese!" she commanded.

The camera snapped again, and now the moment would last forever.

49 Ski's First New Year

By the time the sun sank behind the foothills, four reindeer formed a chorus line in the front yard. Their arms wrapped around each other's shoulders, while stubby legs of snow reached out before them, each decorated with bits of red licorice as painted toenails.

Earlier, Ski and I stopped by a dance in town but found it mostly inhabited by young teens and their parents. After dancing with two or three sixteen-year old girls, we dragged Main Street twice and returned home before ten thirty.

The most striking difference from other nights at Grandma's was that all the kids were still awake. Their screams and shouts shattered what would have been the quiet peace we had grown accustomed to late at night. It seemed appropriate for New Year's Eve, but held none of the excitement and fun of a university dance or celebration downtown in a large city.

While Ski and I had both dreaded the upcoming end of our vacation, we finally realized how starved we were for interaction with people our own age. Thinking about going back to school tomorrow nearly brought the excitement back into the evening.

The noisemakers purchased for midnight went off frequently throughout the house. The kids had found the paper bag full of them in the front closet, and now they enthusiastically tried to catch people off guard and make them jump.

New Year's resolutions were a popular topic of conversation

for a while, but soon it seemed that every idea had been used up. Someone lit a fire in the fireplace, and everyone crowded around to roast marshmallows and make s'mores.

When 11:45 arrived, Uncle Jon got out the short-wave radio from the closet and tuned in to Greenwich Meridian Time. Beeps marked each second and a British accent reported the minutes. Everyone gathered around when the passing year had only one minute left to live, then the countdown began.

"Ten! Nine! Eight! Seven!"

I looked around the room, wishing I had someone nearby to kiss. No such luck.

"Six! Five! Four! Three!"

Many hands secured holds on noisemakers. In the background I heard the old grandfather clock strike its first chime. For a split second, I was transported back exactly one year earlier when I stood on a bridge over the Bear River in Evanston with Annetta, holding her tightly in my arms, watching the fireworks, then kissing her soft lips, her breath blowing warm and gently against my cheek.

For a split second, I felt the heat of her body pressed against mine. I looked into her bright green eyes and the love growing between us rushed into my heart and up through my neck into my head and face.

The old joy rushed forward once again and my heart skipped a beat. I almost gasped. The beginning of tears leapt to my eyes. I would have been stunned at this reaction if it hadn't happened so quickly, if I'd have had enough time to think and analyze it. The split second was so clear that it seemed to last for minutes before the next shout shattered the memory:

"Two!"

My thoughts flew forward to the present, passing through all the months of school and summer and fall. Of missing Annetta and then falling for Julie. Of classrooms and tests, carefree afternoons at the dam, snowfall and rain, sunshine and stunning, star-studded nighttime skies. Of dreams and words and events that now blurred into nothing but a long streak of brilliant color and the left-over feelings it left smeared across my heart.

Everything now looked like the present, but something felt different. Something important had changed. I felt like Jimmy Stewart after the novice angel Charlie had taken him on his tour of an alternate past. Like Ebenezer Scrooge having visited Christmas past, present and future. Something had changed inside me that separated me from this reality.

Before I had a chance to name what had changed, another shout wiped away the unsettling impression and I could not find it nor bring it back.

"One! Happy New Year!!!"

Noise makers popped, tiny streamers filled the air, aunts and uncles smooched, and children scattered as kisses threatened to land on their cheeks. In the background, the grandfather clock finished ringing in the New Year. I slipped out the door to the relative silence of the porch.

It didn't matter what just happened at three seconds till midnight. It didn't matter that Annetta still held a place in my heart. The bittersweet appeal of nostalgia is the result of memories rendered impossible to retrieve, usually sweetened by distance and time. But time moves forward and never back. Ring out the old, ring in the new. I would choose my own life and my own future rather than leave them to undependable fate.

The party continued inside and voices seeped outside through windowpanes. "I resolve not to go to bed tonight!" shouted an eight-year old.

"I resolve that you *will*!" answered his father.

The noisemakers had all gone off and the voices soon wandered upstairs to bed. When all had grown silent, the door behind me opened and Ski stepped onto the porch. He closed the door and gazed up at the clear, star-studded sky.

"Now comes the real test," he said, leaning one shoulder against a wooden pillar.

"What test is that?"

"The clock has struck midnight," Ski answered, scanning the moonlit horizon. "The ball has nearly ended. Will the fairy godmother's spell break? Will the carriage turn back into a pumpkin? Will I no longer be the handsome prince when I leave this palace for home?"

"You will go back to being the mistreated step son and the princess will find you and marry you anyway simply because the shoe fits," I assured him.

"That's the same thing Julie said." I glanced over now, wondering if I had missed a call. "Last week," he clarified. "You mentioned something about me changing, so she made me supply every tiny detail."

"And what do you think?" I asked. "Is the change permanent?"

"For the first time," he replied, " I don't expect this year to be pretty much like the last. The path ahead was always so clear before, all I had to do was follow it. Now I have choices, and for the first time, those choices might matter. Freedom is exciting, but scary, too. Like the world has always been spinning under my feet, but I've never lifted my feet from the path before, and now I'm afraid I might get spun off."

"Any revolution has its price," I said, making a little word play on the cost of freedom and the spinning planet.

"Look at all those stars!" Ski exclaimed, as if noticing them for the first time in his life. "This is my first real *New* Year."

50 New Year's Day

I woke up late again on New Year's Day. This time, no noise flooded under the door from the hallway. Everyone else had stayed up late, too, and they had also slept in. I rolled out of bed and found that Ski gone, his bed made, his bags packed.

I found him in the kitchen with Grandma. They had fixed breakfast together and were just placing the last plates of French toast, bacon, and omelets into the oven to wait for everyone to wake up and make their way downstairs.

"Good morning, Spencer," Grandma said cheerfully.

"Good morning, Spence," Ski added. It was interesting to notice that such a greeting didn't sound out of place coming from him now. Less than two weeks ago that phrase would never have escaped his lips without obvious sarcasm.

"Are you all ready for the drive home?" Grandma asked.

"I don't think I'm ever really ready to leave, Gram," I answered, "but I *am* ready to *get* home."

"Oh, no!" I added quickly. "I'm *not* ready!" If I wasn't ready to slip the diamond ring onto Julie's finger immediately…. "I still need to find her a Christmas present!"

"I wouldn't worry too much," Ski said, "Everything's on sale now, you'll find something."

"Yeah, I guess. Anyway, it's not like I need to find the perfect gift, right?"

"The perfect gift," Grandma quipped, "is the one given with the heart."

The sound of feet on the stairs interrupted our conversation, and everyone soon made their way downstairs.

Everyone else wouldn't leave for home until tomorrow. Ski and I planned to drive away after breakfast. We both wanted to get back to school to beat the long bookstore and financial aid office lines that could eat up hours of our time if we didn't arrive early tomorrow morning.

I packed my things after breakfast and carried them downstairs to the front door, then stepped into the living room to say our goodbyes. Everything in the room looked exactly the same as it had when we arrived, but the atmosphere felt entirely different. The smell of vacation's end hung in the air like the first scents of Spring's arrival in March, and Ski and I both felt restless to get outside and start for home.

"Well, I guess this is it," I announced. Ski started to pull his coat on, but I knew better. Saying goodbye around here was like announcing your own funeral—everyone suddenly tried to think of every last detail they had forgotten to tell you over the course of your life. Last-chance conversations could have carried on for hours if not for the interruptions of others.

The talk finally neared its end and the time came for the hugs. The people who wanted the best hugs waited patiently by the doorway so as not to be hurried by others waiting in line.

"You take care of yourself, Spencer," Grandma ordered as she kissed my cheek. "And don't let your classes get you too busy to call!"

"I won't, Gramma. Thanks for everything."

Alisha was next. "Good bye, big brother..." she said, smiling. I picked her up in a bear hug and we squeezed each other as hard as we could – or at least pretended to.

Ski hugged Grandma and Alisha, saving Diane for last.

"It was a pleasure beating you at Scrabble," Alisha told him.

"Bye, Ski," Diane laughed as he held her tight, picked her up, and spun around in circles.

"Hey! What are you doing?" he joked. "Let go! You're choking me!" he said, spinning faster and faster. Di only squealed and laughed harder.

We finally picked up our bags and walked out to the car. We let the engine warm up for a few seconds before pulling onto the road, waving our last good-byes to everyone who had stepped onto the porch to see us off.

"Now you know why I love 'em so much, eh?" I asked as Ski turned on the stereo. He didn't answer. He only looked at me with

The Perfect Gift

an understanding look, then turned up the volume and turned to stare out the window.

Vacation had all but ended and the real world waited at the other end of the highway.

51 Full Circle

I glanced down and saw the miniature Eiffel Tower sitting next to the car radio. I had forgotten to give it away. I thought momentarily of giving it to Julie, but that wouldn't do. She had never loved French and it would always remind me too much of Annetta.

Instead, I hit the brakes as we passed by Becca's Diner, just before the highway entrance out of Amber, and pulled into the parking lot where Netta and Amy and Jim used to work.

"Didn't I tell you to use the bathroom before we left, kids?" Ski asked, watching me with a mildly curious gaze, wondering what had made me pull off the road so abruptly.

"I'll be right back," I told him, unbuckling my seat belt and stepping out of the car. I carried the tower inside and found the room vacant. Music played from back in the kitchen and I heard the clanking and swishing sounds of dishes being washed. Whoever was back there began singing along with the radio, loud and off key. They obviously hadn't heard me come in.

I walked over to the counter, to the barstool where I first sat down a year ago to order lemonade, near the kitchen door the beautiful Annetta had stepped through to take my order, and where we arranged our first date.

I set the tower down on the bar next to the salt and pepper shakers, then turned and walked back out the door. As I felt the cold air again on my face, I felt the satisfaction of

Shaun Roundy

coming full circle. Here is where it all began, and here is where it finally ends.

People would surely wonder where the tower came from, but they might guess that it had something to do with the Hall girls and keep it around. People who knew and loved them would appreciate the reminder.

Nostalgia burned hot inside my heart, and part of me hated to leave this beautiful little town that time forgot, but the rest of me felt excited to go. Not only would it feel nice to get home and finally see Julie again, but I could leave behind all the conflicting thoughts and feelings stirred up by these familiar surroundings.

"Goodbye," I whispered under my breath as I tugged open the car door.

Goodbye to Amber.

Goodbye to Annetta.

Goodbye to whatever might have been.

52 The Extra Mile

We stopped for gas in Evanston. I filled up the tank and walked inside the station. The attendant sang to himself along with the country music on the radio as I took a look around. This was one of those fancy truck stops, designed for truckers and tourists on their way through Wyoming who wanted a souvenir to prove they had stepped out of their car in the cowboy state.

Racks of humorous post cards, obnoxious baseball caps and bumper stickers, and an art section beckoned with rustic paintings and wood sculptures inside a large glass showcase. Ski had already made his way to the showcase and stood looking through the glass.

"Check out this one of the cougar," he said. The mountain lion was carved from the same dark wood as the stallion Grandma gave me. The swirling grain of the wood added the illusion of motion to the cat. You could almost see its muscles ripple along its flanks as it gathered itself up to pounce.

I had once found fresh cougar tracks in the snow of the nearby mountains. The four-toed prints were as wide as my fist. They fell closely together At first,, but the distance between them jumped to over fifteen feet where the big cat began to run. I followed the tracks for over a mile, trying to imagine what the cougar had looked like, and this sculpture looked exactly how I had pictured it.

"Yeah, that's really nice," I agreed.

The attendant stepped over to the showcase and greeted us with an energetic "Howdy! Would you like to take a look at that?" He looked about sixty and wore a handle bar mustache. I couldn't help thinking that the mustache made the man look a little crazy, as if he had spent too much time alone on the trail and the lone prairie.

The price tag of the sculpture lay strategically upside down so you would fall in love with the carving before finding out its price.

"How much do these run?" I asked.

"Oh, prices vary according to size," he answered ambiguously. He twirled one corner of his mustache and leaned against the counter behind him.

"How much for the cougar, then?"

"Let's see, this one's eighty-five dollars," he said, placing the tag face-down again after looking.

"A bit much for my student budget, I'm afraid," I said as Ski pulled out his wallet to count his money.

The attendant walked back to the register to help a customer and I started toward the restroom when another sculpture caught my eye. It was a pine tree standing on a ridge. The artist had carved intricate detail along the tips of the branches, showing the cones and needles. Other parts of the tree had been sanded perfectly smooth, which created the illusion of snow piled high on the boughs. The dark wood grain swirled perfectly once again, matching the shape of the tree and making you feel like you were watching the ridge through blowing clouds.

The base of the tree was set between two large rocks and a few small trees grazed the edge of the pine. The bottom of the carving was the actual branch that it had been carved from, with no embellishment. The rough knots showing there stood out in contrast with the fine detail of the upper half, and complimented the entire presentation.

"This would make a nice gift for Julie," I thought out loud.

I lowered myself to where I could look up through the glass to read the price tag. "Seventy five bucks," I read. Maybe if I hadn't already bought Julie's ring, I could have afforded this. And I would give her the ring soon enough. I'd have to find her something else for now.

The other customers who had been flipping through the postcards and bumper stickers wandered over and examined the sculpture with us.

"It certainly is beautiful," they said, nodding their appreciation. "If you're not planning to buy it," the woman looked at me questioningly, almost apologetically, "we'd be happy to give it a good home."

As much as I'd have liked to have it, I knew I wouldn't buy it. "Sure," I said. "Go ahead." I left, and when I came back, Ski held a box under his arm. Both the cougar and the pine ridge had vanished from the showcase.

"This cougar's gonna look great in my room," Ski said. "It'll match your stallion perfectly, too." I looked outside through the glass doors and watched the couple drive away with the pine ridge.

"Too bad about the tree thing," Ski added. But there was no use thinking about it more, so we bought a few candy bars and sodas and got back on the road. The attendant was laughing to himself as we walked out the doors. "Alonzo!" he whispered under his breath.

53 Home Sweet Home

Ski and I shuffled through crowds of returning students in the bookstore the next morning and we headed toward the register lines once we had found all our textbooks. Despite the crowds, the relaxed feeling of vacation still lingered. We weren't in a hurry and didn't mind waiting so much.

I thought about picking up Julie at the airport late tonight. Her flight arrived at 11:40. I'd stand there with flowers and resist the desire to run up and give her a bear hug. "Howdy, stranger," I'd say as she approached. Then she would set down her carry-on bag and we would hold each other for a long time. We would stop somewhere for hot chocolate on the way home and talk, laugh, hold hands and bask in how nice it would feel to be together again.

Ski picked up a paperback near the register and began scanning the first chapter. "Nice hat," I told him. He wore Rod's leather hat, now washed, and it looked good.

"Ya think so?" he asked.

"Yeah. Makes you look like some Eastern European military official or something."

Ski nodded and returned to his paperback. I looked over the crowd and eavesdropped on surrounding conversations.

One of the guys in front of me sounded excited for the

The Perfect Gift

quarter to begin. "Carrie's looking hot! I suddenly don't mind being back in school!"

"Not me, man," his friend answered. "Laura's old boyfriend bought her a car stereo for Christmas, and now she's thinking of going back to the jerk."

The couple right behind us didn't seem very happy, either. "I hate these stupid lines," the guy said. "It's bad enough we have to pay so much for tuition and books without having to wait in impossible lines all the time." Before I knew it, Ski struck up a conversation.

"What, you think these long lines?" He spoke with a foreign accent to match his broken grammar. "In my country, this very small line. At least you here don't standing in line for toiletski paper. In my country, we stand in line for everything, then it run out. Yes, is wonderful place, America! Here, you have toilet paper hang from trees!"

"Are you from Russia?" the girl asked, oblivious to Ski's joke.

"Well," Ski began to answer, "is not Russia. Is Ukraine, for being exact."

"Really?" the guy asked, the slightest bit of doubt showing in his expression.

Our friend Adam entered the bookstore just then and headed for the rows of textbooks stacked behind us. He had spent the break at home in Southern California and his tan hinted of cool days at the beach. "Hey, Spencer, hey Ski," he said, slapping Ski on the shoulder as he passed. "Welcome back from the frozen wasteland!" That did the trick. Our new friend, who must have associated anything Russian with the Siberian steppe, became a believer.

"So why did you come to America?" he asked while I turned away to suppress my laughter. Their conversation continued until we reached the register and paid for our books.

"Good luck with your potato farm," they said genuinely. "And we hope you enjoy your stay!" They had entirely forgotten about standing in long, unpleasant lines. Ski shook their hands heartily between both of his.

"I thank you for well wishes. And I hope for you to have *very* nice day!"

Pushing our way through the crowded hallway outside the bookstore, Ski turned to me and confided, "When we said goodbye, I was fighting the strongest urge to grab them by the shoulders and kiss them on both cheeks."

"You should have!" I laughed, and we continued talking as

we walked down the hall. "You in the mood for some hot chocolate and bread?" I asked. "It feels so good to be back in school, I just want to hang out and soak it all in."

"There'll be plenty of time for that later," Ski assured me. "Let's get all this stuff back home and lighten our load."

"Okay," I conceded. I could walk the ten minutes back to campus and the financial aid office after an early lunch. At home, I pulled a can of stew from the cupboard and emptied it into two bowls. Ski carried his books to his room and walked back into the kitchen. "Hey, I got ya something."

I looked up from the microwave and Ski handed me a postcard. It was one of the ones for sale back at the Wyoming gas station and showed a ten-foot-tall jackalope standing next to a VW bug filled with terrified tourists.

"It's beautiful, Ski," I laughed. "Thank you so much!" I turned the card over and saw that Ski had written a message. It read, "Words can not express the value of true friendship, or my unrepayable debt to you, Spencer."

I read it twice and smiled with satisfaction. "Thanks."

We finished lunch and as I rinsed the bowls in the sink, Ski said, "That postcard was a joke." I looked at him with an expression that said, "Of course," and he continued. "It took me a while to decide what you'd really like, but I finally found it. I got the last one."

I looked at him, waiting for understanding to dawn on me. He walked back to his room and returned with the box he had held in the gas station. He set it on the counter and waited. I opened the box slowly, but I already knew what I would find inside. From the wadded tissue paper, I lifted the dark hardwood sculpture of the pine ridge and held it up to the light.

"Ski...!" I began to protest.

"Give it to Julie," he said.

"But, it's..."

"Hey," he interrupted, "it wasn't that much, and what else am I gonna do with all my money?"

"But I thought..."

"They bought the cougar. I told them the artist carved it of his pet cougar, Alonzo."

I paused for a moment. I didn't know what to say. "Thanks, Ski. It's the perfect gift."

Ski looked me in the eye and nodded once. "I was wondering..." he began to say at the same time as I said, "I'll tell her it's from both of us.

"What?" I asked next.

"That's what I was wondering," he answered. "Thanks. Have you noticed the symbolism of that thing?"

I stared at the sculpture and Ski explained.

"That wood grew up all twisted and gnarled because of its environment – the wind, the heavy snow, the cold, and the dry place it probably sprouted. But now the artist comes along, and with his knife, reveals something beautiful that was inside the tree the whole time."

I nodded and thought about Ski's recent transformation and the divine knife that had cut away so much of the old bark. Then, unable to resist, added, "For a tree, you seem to be developing a pretty high opinion of yourself."

"Don't hate me because I'm beautiful," Ski answered, tossing his head to one side like a shampoo model.

54 Home is where the Heart is

The financial aid lines only took an hour, leaving too much time with nothing to do but wait for Julie's flight. I headed home thinking maybe Ski and I could go for a ski up nearby Green Canyon to pass the time, but arrived to find the apartment empty. Instead, I busied myself by finishing unpacking and getting my backpack ready for class in the morning. Finally, with nothing better to do, I lay down on the couch for a quick afternoon nap.

I woke up when the doorbell rang. I got up slowly and walked down the stairs to the door, feeling groggy and still half-asleep. The early afternoon sun shone brightly off the snow and made me squint as I opened the door, but through my half-closed eyelids, what I saw standing on my porch was a beautiful, blue-eyed blonde grinning up at me.

"Julie!" I shouted, stepping forward and throwing my arms around her neck. She hugged me back tightly. "How did you get here?" I asked, pulling away just far enough to look into her bright eyes. "How long have you been back?" Julie wasn't finished smiling at me, enjoying the surprise, and I suddenly noticed the cold and led her inside, closing the door behind us.

Once I had maneuvered her up one step so I could look straight into her eyes, I asked again. "I thought your flight didn't come in till eleven forty! How did you…"

"I told you wrong!" she interrupted. "I read my ticket wrong. My flight came in at eleven forty *a.m.* instead of *p.m.* I'm so sorry!"

We hugged again and I could think of nothing other than how good it felt to see her. Julie finally pushed me away and looked into my eyes again with her hands resting on my shoulders, then slid her hands behind my neck, pulled me forward, and kissed me in a long, soft embrace. I wrapped my arms around her waist and held her body against me until she pulled away and took my hands in hers.

"I had forgotten how handsome you are," she said, sounding surprised and pleased. "Come on," she said next, leading me upstairs to sit down on the couch. "We have some getting reacquainted to do."

We sat down and I draped my arm around her shoulders, but just as I began to pull her closer, she leaned back suddenly and her eyes widened. "What have you done to Ski?!" she asked incredulously, her eyes growing suddenly round in surprise.

"How do you know about…?"

"He picked me up from the airport," Julie interrupted. "I didn't remember I had told you my flight time wrong until I had already boarded the plane. So I called as soon as I landed, but you didn't answer, so I called your apartment and he was the only one home."

My cell battery had died during the weeks of non-use in Amber, and I had left it charging on my desk this morning.

"He said he could run up to campus and find you, but I told him it would be more fun to surprise you." Her eyes sparkled as she remembered the shock that must have shown on my face when I opened the door, then crawled forward again, wrapped her arms around my neck and kissed me again. When she stopped, she slid over so she sat half on my lap and half leaned against the arm of the couch, keeping one arm around my neck as she ran her fingers lightly through my hair.

We sat on the couch and talked for hours, until it grew dark, stopping only long enough for dinner. I told her stories about the family and the snow, about snowmobiling and the changes I witnessed in Ski. I gave her her present and explained the symbolism Ski told me about.

Any memories of Annetta seemed distant and irrelevant now, just as I had hoped they would. Julie talked about the time she spent wandering along the windy, cold sea shore, loosing herself among drifting sand dunes and beached drift wood, imagining it was drifting snow instead, and that the driftwood was actual trees protruding above the snow pack.

Ski finally came home sometime before midnight, having considerately left us alone all day long. Julie and I decided we'd better get some sleep and finish catching up tomorrow. She gave me a quick kiss as she stood up and gave Ski a long, strong hug as she walked toward the door. "Welcome home," she told us both, then opened the door and left.

In my room, on my desk, inside a small red box, sat the perfect gift, just waiting for the right moment to be given away. I wouldn't have to wait much longer.

55 Life Goes On

The semester began in the morning and soon we each grew busy with classes and homework. Even so, the three of us found plenty of time to spend together skiing, talking and laughing over lunch on campus, and watching movies and then discussing them until late into the night.

Ski no longer seemed uncomfortable around us and his transformation continued to solidify. His confidence grew and his humor slowly changed from mostly sarcastic wit to something with less of a sharp edge to it.

He still taunted Ben for his self-centeredness and over-intellectualization of every topic, but putting him down ceased to be a main focus in his life. He still occasionally fabricated stories and forced us to play along, but he laughed more often and his inventions more often made people laugh along and less often made them look like fools.

"Latrina," he said to Julie with a mild southern drawl, pointing to a girl in the row behind us as we sat down in the movie theater one evening, "ain't that the girl you said you'd like to rassle fer her shoes?"

"No, Jimmy Joe," Julie replied without missing a beat. "I said I'd like to ask her who made them."

The girl's expression went from mildly shocked to merely guarded, and she told Julie the brand.

"Well I don' think she's funny lookin' at'all," Ski tried next, implying that Julie had said so.

"'Course you don't, she looks very nice. Now you turn around and behave yerself."

Ski seemed comfortable discussing topics he had previously avoided. He still didn't have much to say about his parents, but he started attending church with Julie.

"How was church?" I asked one Sunday afternoon.

"Fine," he replied.

"Do you have any opinion about God and religion yet?" I probed.

"I noticed an interesting feeling there," he admitted, "and I liked it, but I'm going to experiment more before I take anything too seriously."

Experimenting, as it turned out, meant, in part, prayer.

"You look happy," I noted one morning as Ski walked into the kitchen with a bright light shining in his eyes.

"I was just talking to God," Ski told me, and after a pause, added, "and I think he may have said something back."

I nodded approvingly.

"I have no idea what, though," Ski said, looking perplexed.

"Sometimes He just wants to let you know He's there and he loves you," I explained.

Ski nodded and proceeded to pour a bowl of cereal.

56 Two Weeks

Two weeks passed and I still hadn't proposed to Julie. Somehow the right moment hadn't yet arrived. Our relationship changed as we spent so much time with Ski. With his sly wit constantly around, our interactions grew less serious and romantic and more playful. I began to get to know a side of Julie that I hardly noticed before.

Even when Julie and I spent time alone, the tone seemed reluctant to shift back. Julie seemed happier than ever, but I missed our old relationship. But everything would work out. I could be patient.

One night I made up my mind to propose. I would ask her to marry me, and she would say yes, and then everything would return to the way it had been, or better. I took Julie to dinner at the nicest restaurant in town, and over dessert, just as I reached into my pocket for the ring, she suddenly excused herself and went to the ladies room.

Minutes later when she returned, the mood wasn't right. We left the restaurant and I steered toward the dam, one of our favorite places last summer, suggesting that we go for a walk on the ice. Once there, Julie kept saying how beautiful and fun it was, but also how cold she felt as she shuffled along to keep warm. I couldn't get her to stop and look in my eyes, and the right moment never came.

57 One Month

A month passed and I walked into my room one night, opened the red felt box to stare at the diamond, and wondered if the right time would ever come.

Ski had declined our invitation to join us for dinner that evening, and when we asked why, he explained that he was having an unusually rough day and he would rather spend it alone than bring us down.

"Madison Ski!" Julie scolded immediately. "That's when you need your friends the most!" She sat down next to him on the couch and gave him a long hug, waiting for him to hug her back, waiting for his small frown to transform into a happy, silly grin.

"That's better," she affirmed. "Now then, tell me what's wrong."

Ski didn't know what was wrong, so Julie peppered him with questions about his feelings until they began to figure it out and work through it, replacing old limited perceptions with a new vision full of opportunity and freedom.

Half an hour later, the conversation had clearly only begun, so I offered to pick up some burgers while they continued.

I returned and listened in for a while, but eventually wandered into my room to focus on homework.

"Did Julie fill you up with enough happy thoughts last night?" I asked Ski the next morning.

"It's not just about thinking happy thoughts," Ski explained, "first you have to get a really good grip on something positive, and then keep holding on while feeling the old negative ones, too, so the old ones blend in and transform permanently instead of just sweeping them under the carpet."

58 Four Months

Two months passed and I felt seriously concerned. Something was happening. Tonight the three of us had watched an old movie and, for the first time, Julie had not kissed me goodnight. She gave me the same strong hug she gave Ski before walking out the door. I tried to follow her outside to her car, but she turned and hugged me again, then said a very final-sounding "Good night" and turned again and left.

Three months passed, and one day, without ever discussing it, I realized that Julie was not my girlfriend anymore. She had probably known this for weeks. I felt confused and betrayed and sometimes didn't feel like hanging out with both Julie and Ski. It had grown too late to object, too late to ask for things to go back to how they had been before, and now Ski and Julie had begun spending time together alone.

Four months passed and one day Ski came home and went straight to his room, then avoided talking to me for days.

I finally decided to confront Julie and ask exactly what had happened between us and what we might expect in the future. I felt foolish about it now, as if I should have seen exactly what had happened, that I was yesterday's news and only tagging along like an unwanted puppy dog.

I knew better than to think I wasn't appreciated. I knew I was still loved by both of them in some special way, and I hoped that a long-overdue talk might clear the air and make things feel more comfortable again.

I still hadn't returned the diamond ring. I still hoped that something might work out, that conditions might improve, and besides, I wasn't sure the store would let me return it after such a long time.

"Let's go for a walk," Julie suggested when I requested the talk. Spring had arrived, warmer breezes spilled from the canyon mouth in late morning, green leaves rolled out of bud all around the valley, and the snow had entirely melted away from the canyon floors.

I climbed into Julie's car and she drove us up the canyon. We crossed the bridge at Third Dam, parked her car, and meandered down-canyon along a dirt road next to the river. Neither of us spoke for a while as we thought about what words to begin with.

"Something's happening," Julie finally began, "between Ski and I."

146   The Perfect Gift

All the words I had been preparing instantly became pointless. Now there was no more use talking about "us." Everything about "us" had just been irreversibly relegated to the past.

We walked along in silence for a while longer, Julie with her slightly pained expression, her concern for me written clearly across her face; me with the pain and disappointment screaming inside my head that I tried my best to conceal.

"What happened, anyway?" I finally asked, partly just to make Julie speak and draw attention away from the oppressive silence.

Julie's dam of words broke then and she spoke in gushing sentences about how she had a crush on Ski from the first time he ever approached her, spoke with her and invited her to our study session over a year ago. She explained how the feeling had grown while she spent time with him over Christmas break, but that she had also seen that pursuing a relationship with him would be impossible, that something inside him made his heart inaccessible.

She talked about how highly Ski had spoken of me, and how when I returned from the break, she had found that everything Ski told her was true. She spoke of falling in love with my kind heart and love of nature. "You've changed me forever, do you know that?" she asked. "I never realized how incredibly beautiful the world was until you showed me how to see it."

Next, Julie related in greater detail her soul searching over Christmas break and why she spent so much time wandering among the dunes at the beach. She realized that I was planning to propose to her soon and she wanted to make sure that our relationship would be everything she wanted for herself.

"It sounds cold, I know," she admitted, "and maybe a little heartless, to even be able to think about that sort of thing when we were getting along so well, but I knew I had to do whatever I thought was best, and I knew I had to be careful and choose my way with my heart *and* my head.

"What I decided," she continued, looking off toward the surrounding trees and gray limestone cliffs, "was that yes, we were everything I could ever ask for. I decided that I loved you and we could be happy and continue to grow together forever."

Her words surprised me and brought back all the anguish of loss and confusing feelings of betrayal.

"So I flew home all ready to marry you and live happily ever after, when…." Her voice trailed off as she reached the difficult part of her story. "And then there was Ski. And he was so different. And he had this new light in his eyes. And suddenly I could connect to him and to his heart. And I felt so happy and excited for him! And for the longest time I didn't notice, but…just being around him completes me in a way I've never known before.

"I still expected you to propose and for us to live happily ever after and weeks passed and I wondered why you were taking so long, and by the time we went to the restaurant…"

"You knew I was going to propose there?" I asked.

Julie grimaced sympathetically. "Yes. And at the dam."

I nodded. "And you purposefully didn't let me ask."

"You hadn't seemed as sure about us," she explained. "And I wanted to wait until you seemed sure again."

So this was my fault, I realized. My hesitation had ruined everything. If I hadn't thought so much about Annetta and hesitated as a result, Julie and I would have gotten engaged within days of coming home.

"And then, recently," Julie continued, "I started noticing Ski in a way I never expected. I started noticing how happy he makes me."

Julie used to always tell me that *I* made her happy. I had been replaced. Julie's words stung, but I fought not to let it show.

"And I thought, maybe…I should pay attention to those feelings. And I argued with myself for a long time, because I still thought you were better for me in so many important ways. You're so thoughtful and good and I knew I would always be safe and well cared for.

"I didn't know what to do! So I decided to give things time and see what happened. And what finally happened was…that something started happening between Ski and I. And I finally saw that he is what I need most. And I know that we'll have our trials and challenges together, but that somehow facing them together, all that doesn't matter so much, ya know?"

Julie paused then and looked up at me, hoping for some sort of reassurance that I understood and accepted her decision.

"Well," she continued after I didn't return her gaze or say anything in response, "you can't imagine how uncomfortable this made Ski and I feel. I mean, you are our dearest friend! We both owe you so much! And after everything we've been through together…I guess I still don't know exactly what to do."

"You have to do what you feel is best," I said bluntly, stopping in the trail and finally looking her in the eye momentarily.

"So all's fair in love and war?" she asked after a brief pause.

"No, it's not," I countered. "It's not fair. Nothing is ever fair, but that's beside the point, isn't it? You have to do what you think is best."

Julie looked a bit stunned momentarily at what was surely the most abrupt tone of voice I had ever used toward her. We both began walking down the road in silence again, and I could tell by the way her shoulders seemed to relax that her confusion was clearing up and that I had finally set her free.

I wanted to run. I wanted to shout, I wanted to scream out all the frustration and pain searing through my heart, but I had no idea what I would say. I wanted to get away from Julie and the terrible, oppressive thundering thoughts booming through my head.

"I am so sorry, Spencer," she said a minute later, taking my hand for the first time in weeks. "I hope you know that I meant what I told you, that I will always lo…"

"I know it," I cut her off, pulling my hand out of hers. I knew it, I knew she would always love me, but I didn't want to hear her say the words. Not now. Not ever again.

59 The Darkest Hour

A few days later, I came home from class and passed Ski on his way out. We seemed to cross paths this way often and I wondered if he did it on purpose, not wanting to face the discomfort between us, probably not knowing what to say and not wanting to make things any worse for me than they already were.

I didn't know what to say either, so I didn't say anything. I couldn't blame him or Julie. I could only blame myself.

"Something interesting just arrived for you," he said, slapping me on the shoulder as he passed.

"See ya later," I said as he trotted down the stairs and outside.

School would end in two weeks. We would all graduate and go our separate ways. Then Ski wouldn't have to put on a show of casual, nonchalant friendship—the only façade I had ever seen him fail to portray convincingly.

We would remain friends, but at a distance. Someday, in the distant future, the discomfort between us would pass. Everything would stop mattering and all would be forgotten. We would send

Christmas cards to each other's families and get together to let our kids play with each other every year or two.

I wandered over to the counter and found a blue airmail envelope sitting atop the small pile of bills and junk mail. The stamp and postmark were French.

I didn't dare believe the obvious truth. Annetta had finally written back. I turned the envelope over and sure enough, I still recognized the address even after all this time. Hall. Rue de Septembre, 17. Marseilles, France.

I quickly moderated the hope that momentarily flared up in my heart. Nothing would change. Annetta wouldn't come crawling back to me after a full year of silence. Perhaps this was a wedding announcement and she decided to forgive past grievances so she could start her new life with a clear conscience.

I recognized that I was being ridiculous. We couldn't start up where we left off, but at least she had sent a letter. At least she had shown some sort of effort. I should feel grateful. I should feel excited and curious about what she would have to say to me after all this time.

Maybe Jim had heard about Julie and I breaking up through the grapevine and passed the word along. Maybe that had been enough to induce her to finally break her vow of silence.

All these thoughts flashed through my mind in an instant and then my mind settled onto the caboose of this train of thought – who cares? What does it matter? What does anything matter?

I carried the letter to my room and dropped it on my desk along with my backpack, and lay down on the bed. My curtains hung open and I stared outside at the green mountains glowing as the warm afternoon sunlight spilled across their smooth contours.

Life is hard, I thought, and then, *If only….*

If only I had played my hand differently. If only I had proposed to Julie the night we said goodbye after finals. If only I had listened to my head and not let myself remember Annetta. If only I had proposed the minute Julie and I got back together. If only my lucky star had held on for a few days or weeks or months longer.

And when things didn't work out…I should have let go sooner, as soon as I saw us growing apart. I should have adapted more quickly, but nothing mattered now. *What's done is done.*

I had no right to expect everything to fall into my lap simply because I wanted it to. Julie and Ski were smart enough to take the best path once they knew it. They were kind enough to struggle with the decision for a long time first. They had done everything right and I couldn't have fairly advised them to do anything differently.

Even so, I couldn't help letting that reflect on my own self-image. If I could be let go of so quickly, what did that say about my value? What did that reveal about what I really have to offer, when the one relationship I had ever been willing to give everything to failed because I wasn't good enough?

But all that had ended. Nothing mattered anymore. I would let it go as soon as possible. I would move on, too, and eventually find someone else to love, and then I would be happy, and then I would forget, and then it *really* wouldn't matter anymore.

Someday I would even convince myself that the whole past year and a half was a wonderful, though temporary, fairy tale, and that I was fortunate to have experienced it.

I reached over and picked up the letter from the desk and held its light-weight paper between my finger tips for a moment before tearing one edge and extracting the letter. I unfolded the airmail paper began to read.

Dear Spencer,
    That was quite the bold letter you wrote—I like the new you!

What? The only letter I had written for months was the one I scribbled out in the Amber library, the one I had tossed in the trash next to Mr. Milligan's desk on the way out…which explained everything.

Mr. Milligan would have assumed it had fallen off his desk by accident, picked it up, and mailed it anyway.

You're going to have to forgive me for reading your letter because...you have no choice.

What? Why should I forgive her for reading a letter addressed to her? I flipped the paper over and looked at the last line. Sure enough, the name there was not Annetta, but Amy.

So Netta hadn't written me after all. I was right to not get my hopes up.

I didn't know it was from you, anyway. There was no return address, just an Amber postmark, so I assumed it was just another Christmas card for everyone.
    But I'm glad I read it! And Spencer, you should have written

me sooner if Netta wasn't writing back! What's up with forgetting your second best friend in the whole world?? I should say first best – Netta's being such a brat. Oh, yeah, and sorry for not writing to you sooner, too. Oops!

Anyway, I liked how honest you were about everything, but Spencer! What's this about another girl??? You can't give up on my sister! That would be tragic, because if you marry someone else, then you would never have ME for a sister-in-law!!! Tragic!!

Well, once I read your letter and found out what's going on (I can't believe my stupid sister never told us!) I made her explain everything.

I know, she's stubborn. I know, she's a BRAT!! But she's still so awesome, don't you think? And she has those pretty green eyes and everything, right? And hey, you got past her stubbornness once before, so why not do it again? There's no reason to take her little attitudes too seriously.

I've started teasing her about you now (and I don't know if it helps or hurts, but it's fun!) I ask her if she's written to her boyfriend lately and At first, she got annoyed at me and mad and so I said, 'just proves you're still in love!' and now she tells me to shut up or tries not to show any reaction at all, and that's how I know I'm right.

She actually did have a boyfriend here for a while. He was an okay guy, but I kept reminding her about you and she finally broke up with him. Ha! She would never in a million years admit that I had anything to do with it, though!

Here's something else you never knew: everyone except me was surprised when she fell for you last year. Not because you're not great and all, everyone liked you lots, but because Netta had determined not to date anyone in Amber.

She said it was because she was leaving so soon anyway and didn't want to get tangled up in anything she'd just have to leave behind anyway. She won't admit this, but she just made that up as an excuse not to get serious with Jim. She was so stubborn that she thought she had to stand by her words just because she had said them, but you were too irresistible!

But when we moved away and she couldn't look into your gorgeous blue reassuring eyes, and when you started hanging out with that other girl, she got scared of getting hurt, and that's why she stopped writing. She said she might as well cut her losses. And then I said she was <u>soooo</u> stupid! And then she wouldn't talk to me about it anymore.

So much for courage!!! And get this: she's being extra stubborn this time in not writing you and I figured out that it's because she's trying to make up for being less stubborn last year! Is that the stupidest thing you've ever heard or what?!!!

So here's my point: she still likes you. She would never admit this and I don't care if she knows I told you so. And here's the big news that made me finally write you—we just decided to move home this year! Netta's going back to San Diego for her master's next spring, and I'm going to be a freshman there! Cool, huh? I can't wait.

So listen, you've got to build some bridges quick so you two are talking by the time we arrive. What if she met some other dork there and didn't marry you? Once she sees you, she'll be forced by your irresistible charm and dashing good looks to forget all about anything she thinks she's decided.

I guess I'm assuming a lot that you're still interested in her and all—but I know you must be smarter than she is. If not, then at least be open to the idea, okay?

And if you already married that other girl, then...darn it! You better not have! At least try to give it one more chance, okay? If you don't, you'll always regret it when you wonder what might have been.

And if you DID marry that girl, then... congratulations and I'm so happy for you and all those other polite lies. ☺

Other than that, France has been really cool! We can all speak French really well and it's fun to just take off and get around on our own. We went on vacation to Spain last summer and spent an entire month in a little town on the Mediterranean with a castle up on this hill overlooking the sea. We go up to Paris all the time—it's only a few hours away. I got a little trinket for you there, by the way. I'll send it to you later. It's just one of those dumb little Eiffel Tower paperweight things.

And I'm sending you a poem I wrote for Easter this year. I like it! It's about heroes, so I'm sure you'll identify with it.

Anyway, I could go on and on with all the details, but that's the important stuff. Always remember that you are still my hero and I love you and so does my retarded sister. See you this fall!!! I can hardly wait! You are the coolest. Don't forget us, okay?

De gros bisous (that's French for XOXO)

Amy

I reread Amy's letter again and half way through, realized that I was smiling. Then I unfolded a small piece of colored paper and read Amy's poem:

The Darkest Hour

Always Darkest Before the Dawn.
Always silent before the song.
Always coldest before the spring,
But oh, what rich treasures such trials can bring!

When you think you're ready to give up hope,
When you've reached the end of a long, thin rope,
When trying once more doesn't make any sense,
That's the moment that makes all the difference.

That's the moment you can choose to give in
Or the moment you start to fight and to win.
And whatever you choose in this short, golden hour
Will determine your fate when you stand tall or cower.

It's in moments like these when great heroes are born
Who refuse to be beat, though they're bleeding and torn.
Who refuse to admit that the battle is lost,
Who refuse to surrender, no matter the cost.

It's in moments like these when the world makes you shrink
That your actions record as with paper and ink
Whether you'll be the coward with no name and no face
Or a hero whose heart time can never erase.

It's in moments like these that the fate of the earth
Will rest on the shoulders of heroes whose birth
Could never have happened and never been spawned
If not for the dark in the hour before dawn.

I think of the Savior, lifted up on the cross,

There to pay for my sins at a terrible cost.
I think of the nails and the blood that He shed
That He might die, resurrect, and redeem all the dead.

That my soul might be saved through the blood of the Lamb -
The Glorious Jehovah! The Eternal "I Am"!
Who cried out in anguish "Let this cup pass from me,"
But shrank not, though He trembled, and from Hell set us free.

So I'll keep His example and I'll walk where He trod.
I'll pursue the strait path to the Kingdom of God.
When I rise through the clouds once my race has been run,
He will lovingly whisper, "My servant, well done."

60 The End

Ski and Julie took long walks in the canyon and talked for hours in subdued voices at the library where they meant to study together. By July they were dating seriously. They laughed together all the time and Ski grew happier than he ever thought possible.

Such joy sometimes pushed Ski so far from his former comfort zone that he tried to slide back into distance and sarcasm, but he could never succeed. The change had integrated too deeply into his core. There's no such thing as going backward, only forward. The old Ski had vanished forever.

Julie and Ski often invited me to join them for dinner and movies or concerts and other activities. At first, I rejected their invitations, but later accepted occasionally. I realized that I had been wrong the day I spoke with Julie in the canyon – perhaps all is fair in love after all, and spending time with this new reality would help me accept the facts and make the transition.

Julie continued to change in subtle ways because of her relationship with Ski. Her conversation grew wittier, her affection grew more intellectual and less tender (at least the part I witnessed), and the day I realized I was no longer in love with her was a bittersweet, confusing day.

From then on, though, life grew easier and I knew I would eventually move on and find another chance at love. "Time," I told myself. "Give it time."

I still hadn't decided what to think of Annetta. I occasionally began new email messages or pulled out a pen and tried to write to her, but each effort wound up in the trash.

I eventually decided to give up on her, for now. I told myself that I had too much self-respect to beg. If we were to have a second chance, either she would have to write first or we'd have to see each other again and decide what we wanted and where to go from there.

We all graduated and Ski and Julie moved to Oregon where they got engaged early that summer. I got a job in Salt Lake City and occasionally fought the traffic to go hiking or mountain biking in the canyons.

From high above the valley, I would look out across the smog and wonder what was the meaning of life. On bad days, I wondered if life truly had any meaning or if it was just something to be endured.

I made new friends but kept many thoughts and feelings to myself. I didn't want to discuss my discouraging experiences and admit to my mild depression, especially when I didn't trust anyone to understand or be able to help.

I didn't know what I could have done differently with my last two relationships, and I didn't want to move on and risk going through similar disappointments again without finding some answers first.

I often sat on the cool dirt trail high above the valley and thought about my wins and losses. On bad days, I wondered if I had any control over my life and destiny, and if further effort to reach my goals was worth the trouble. If my best efforts led to failure, then why not sit still and wait for time to pass and fate to carry me to my destination without any more effort and hopes and wishes and dreams and disappointments?

To give up would be another gamble, I knew. Risking nothing would diminish my chance at winning anything. Playing it safe was far too dangerous. I may as well keep on trying. All I could lose in the end was the effort, and in the end at least I would know that I tried my best and that I had not given up. This thought gave me a measure of courage and determination.

"Time," I told myself. "Give it time."

Ski and Julie often messaged to see how I was doing. Their gratitude for the part I played in their lives would never fade, they assured me. And they worried about me. They never came out and said as much, but I read it between the lines.

These were true friends, but I never told them much about how I felt. I had played a part in giving each of them the perfect gift - for Ski, my loyal friendship, a few insights, and an environment filled with enough love to allow him to heal; and for Julie, the new-and-improved Ski and her freedom. Now I didn't want to intrude on their perfect happiness by admitting that part of its price was my current loneliness and depression.

"Time," I told myself. "Give it time."

As autumn came on, I felt a little better. The old heaviness that had settled into my lungs dissipated little by little. I saw the past more clearly and everything seemed to make a little more sense.

I came to believe that everything had turned out exactly the way it was meant to. Fate had simply used me for its own ends. Ski-and-Julie was an inevitable combination. Heaven had watched carefully over them, and I could trust it to do the same for me, eventually.

In the meantime, several unanswerable questions ran through my mind. Had the memories of Netta only been placed momentarily in my path to make me let go of Julie when the right time came, or did we have more history in store?

I had no way of knowing, and no way of finding out if Netta never wrote back, especially if I never finished and sent her another message.

Tonight I've come to the high trail with a pen and notepad in my jacket pocket. I take them out and begin to write another letter. This time I will finish. This one I will send to France. I have a new idea this time, a new strategy.

This time I know my efforts will not fail. This time I know I will get a letter in response and I know that letter will be filled with encouraging words and happy news to make me smile.

The evening air feels cool against my bare legs, flowing down the mountainside in a soft breeze. I hold my hand out at arm's length to measure the remaining daylight. The sun hangs three finger-widths above the horizon, leaving forty-five minutes for me to finish the letter and ride back down the trail before dark.

I uncap my pen and begin to write.

Dear Amy...

The End
of book two

What Happens Next?

3. The Art of Heart

The trilogy concludes with book three, which is the best book of all! All loose ends are about to get tied up - but not without tying a few new knots to untie first! It's packed with many unpredictable plot twists and surprises, thrilling action and adventure (based on a true story), inspiring character arcs, and dozens of life-changing insights.

For example, lives are again at risk and heroes must step up to save them, romance rolls the plot over and over in surprising yet believable ways, and Spencer discovers, with a little help from Amy, his greatest weakness. Never give up. From the highest of highs to the lowest lows, there is always hope.

bit.ly/artheart3

Also enjoy the audiobook version of The Art of Heart Christmas Trilogy!

bit.ly/christmasaudiobook
bit.ly/christmasaudiobook2
bit.ly/christmasaudiobook3
bit.ly/christmasaudiobook123

Contents

An American in China
Starting Over

Shaun left in March for a spontaneous six-month voyage through the Orient. Six months later, he didn't return. What did he expect to find by leaving everything behind? His path carries him into the salt spray of dangerously high seas, through frothy, typhoon-swollen rivers, and below shattered, crumbling mountainsides that come crashing down around his feet. Passion for living offered no alternatives.

This journey carries him on motorcycles through crowded city streets and wide-open tropical island beaches, on trains rolling for days across the world's most populous country, starting over again and again and again, discovering what it truly means to live, and what living truly costs. Shaun's engaging writing style will pull you straight into living the adventure. Gather a lifetime of experience in 168 action-packed, heavily illustrated pages. Sometimes it takes a journey of 20,000 miles to finally arrive at one's own heart. Find your ticket to the journey inside An American in China: Starting Over.

Paperback and Kindle: <u>bit.ly/chinaguide</u>

Deep Questions: Know Thyself & The Road of Life

Who asks questions anymore? Smart people, that's who! Interesting people. People worth knowing, and worth keeping around.

The 101 conversation-starter questions inside, plus ~900 follow-up questions, will help you understand yourself more thoroughly, and thereby make the most of your life.

For maximum value, discuss the questions with others to quickly form far deeper and more satisfying connections than you're accustomed to experiencing. You'll wish you made a habit of asking questions, rather than mostly expressing your opinions, years sooner!

<u>UofLIFE.com/books</u>

True You

The Simple Art of Seeing Who You Really Are

Have you ever wondered why eye contact makes people feel uncomfortable? Because it makes you feel exposed, that's why! But why should it make you feel so vulnerable? Are the eyes truly the window to the soul? Can the secret to your true nature be discovered through those tiny stained-glass portals? The definitive answer is: Yes!

The important question is: what will you do about it? Why not dive right in and find out who you really are and who you're meant to become?

Your deep identity has much to offer. It's ready and waiting to show you how to experience your true nature. You'll quickly discover that you are much, much better than anyone told you. You'll develop and experience greater confidence, happiness, satisfaction, purpose, and meaning in life than you ever expected to attain.

bit.ly/trueyoubooks

The Happiness Equation

25 Deep Thoughts & Proven Methods for Catching & Keeping Happiness

The Happiness Equation teaches you many proven methods to increase your happiness easily, deeply, immediately, and permanently. Engaging stories and illustrations introduce concepts and make them memorable, while workshop-style discussion points and action items deepen your grasp. All happiness is not created equal. Three crucial continuums help you measure which kinds are the best and which are worth pursuing.

bit.ly/happyeq

How to Love Yourself

This Love 301 course from the University of Love not only explains clearly and simply exactly what love is and how it works, it also includes self-love tests to reveal how much room for improvement you have, plus enlightening essays followed by discussion questions, application exercises, commitments to make, and other homework and resources to help you effectively internalize this most valuable of all abilities.

bit.ly/self-love-book

The Motivation Equation

50 Deep Thoughts & Proven Methods for Getting Things Done the Easy Way

The space between getting things done and doing nothing (or doing something else) is usually a lot smaller than you ever imagined. Each story in these 50 chapters illustrates vital aspects of motivation and explains how to easily transform resistant inaction into willing action.

bit.ly/motequation

Heal Your Emotions

Practical Guide to Speaking Your Brain's Languages and Turning Pain into Power

This 320-page book walks you through hundreds basic intuitive energy healing techniques that teach you to work *with* your brain rather than against it as most people do.

As your fears and limitations release, you accelerate your progress toward happiness, peace, clarity, abundance, and your true, glorious potential.

bit.ly/healemotions

About the Author

Shaun Roundy earned an MA in English from Utah State University and taught writing there and at Utah Valley University for 15 years.

He has published fourteen books and written various articles and short stories.

Shaun was born in New Jersey, then moved to Massachussettes, California and Brazil before settling in the Rocky Mountains in Logan, Utah.

He later moved to Spain, Taiwan, China, and Utah Valley, as well as working and traveling in many other states and countries, including four months in Honduras and a five-week, 2,500 mile sailing voyage to help a friend bring his boat home from Venezuela.

Shaun enjoys spending time in the outdoors, climbing, mountaineering, camping, skiing, sailing, motorcycling, writing, teaching, learning, video production and more.

He has volunteered on the Utah County Sheriff Search and Rescue team for 19 years, as well as chairing the Mountain Rescue Association's Intermountain Region for 23 years.

He has been interviewed on NPR's *All Things Considered*, and appeared in the Discovery Channel's *Raging Planet - Blizzards* and KUED's award-winning *Secrets of the Lost Canyon* and *Search and Rescue*.

Most of all, Shaun craves beauty, experience, wisdom, fun and adventure, and hopes to share that and make the world a better place.